I Need a Hero

BY
V A BROWNING

EDITED BY:

TRACY SEYBOLD

TRACY@EDITINGBYTRACY.COM

ALL RIGHTS RESERVED.

NO PART OF THIS PUBLICATION MAY BE COPIED, REPRODUCED IN ANY FORMAT, BY ANY MEANS, ELECTRONIC OR OTHERWISE, WITHOUT PRIOR CONSENT FROM THE COPYRIGHT OWNER AND PUBLISHER OF THIS BOOK.

THIS BOOK IS A WORK OF FICTION.

ANY NAMES, CHARACTERS, PLACES, BRANDS, MEDIA AND INCIDENTS EITHER ARE THE PRODUCT OF THE AUTHOR'S IMAGINATION OR ARE USED FICTITIOUSLY. ANY RESEMBLANCE TO SIMILARLY NAMED PLACES OR TO PERSONS LIVING OR DECEASED IS UNINTENTIONAL.

© VA BROWNING, 2013

HTTP://WWW.VABROWNING.COM/

Table Of Contents

Chapter 1	5
Chapter 2	15
Chapter 3	29
Chapter 4	45
Chapter 5	63
Chapter 6	85
Chapter 7	91
Chapter 8	93
Chapter 9	101
Chapter 10	105
Chapter 11	109
Chapter 12	117
Chapter 13	123
Chapter 14	129

Chapter 15	139
Chapter 16	145
Chapter 17	151
Chapter 18	157
Chapter 19	165
Chapter 20	175
Chapter 21	185
Chapter 22	193

Chapter 1

Mike Becker saw the wreck as soon as he crested the hill. The silver Lexus was smashed all to hell, but the telephone pole wasn't hurt too badly. He hoped it was not a fatality. He quickly pulled his truck over and stopped, jumping out and wishing he had his medical bag with him. As he ran toward the car, small flames erupted beneath the front end. The woman in the driver's seat had been knocked unconscious, her head bashed against the car door window. He quickly tried the door, but it would not open.

Standing back, he kicked the window with all his might. He didn't have time for anything else.

The window broke, and her body slumped away with the force. He felt her neck for a pulse and found it, even though it was very faint. Mike's heart raced as he worked quickly to save her. He acted without thought, his medical training keeping him focused. He grabbed the door handle and opened it, then quickly cut the seat belt open with his pocketknife.

Taking a deep breath, he reached under her and gingerly pulled her away from the seatback and cradled her head. *Calm down, Mike, you can do this. Just get her to the hospital.*

He ran toward his truck, reaching it as the car erupted in a fiery blast that pushed him forward. He struggled to hold on to her and not fall. Running around to the other side to shield them from any flying parts, he tried to open his door. After several pulls, he finally got the door opened.

He pushed his groceries off the backseat onto the floor with one fell swoop and gently laid her down. While he was tending to the girl, he noticed a small brown and tan longhaired Yorkshire terrier following him. The dog must have been in the car with her.

Mike took another deep breath and made sure she still had a heartbeat. As he felt for a pulse, he turned her face toward him and really looked at her. His heart was in his throat, and not just from the adrenaline rush of saving her. Her bloodied forehead, chestnut hair, and petite frame made her appear so fragile. If he hadn't been driving by, she'd be dead right now. She was dressed in jeans and a T-shirt, her arms were scraped, and her jeans were torn. He lifted her eyelid, and her pupil reacted to the light. That was a good thing. The cut on her forehead was deep but not that bad. She would need stitches.

He jumped into the driver's seat, and the little dog followed him. As he started driving away, the dog scrambled to the backseat to be with her. Picking up his phone, he dialed 911.

"911, what is your emergency?" the 911 dispatcher Sherry asked calmly.

"This is Mike Becker. I'm on my way to Big Sky Memorial Hospital with an unidentified woman from a car wreck on Highway 9 near Mountain View Road. I need an ambulance to meet me on Highway 9. I'm in my truck and headed north with her. She's in bad shape, with a head injury and possible internal injuries."

"No problem, Dr. Mike. Flash your lights when you see them coming so they know to pull over."

"Thanks, Sherry. Tell the sheriff the wreck was about half a mile south of Mountain View Road and the car was on fire. You should probably send a fire truck."

Big Sky Hospital was not well equipped to handle trauma patients, and he was determined to stay by her side until he knew she was ok.

The agonizingly slow trip had his nerves on edge, so he passed the time trying to figure out who she was. No one around the area owned a silver Lexus. Who was she? He guessed they'd know when she woke up...

He had dealt with trauma for the last ten years, but he was out of practice. Serious doubts ran through his mind. *Should I have moved her? Should I have stayed at the accident scene and waited? Will she be able to recover from the serious head injury?*

The ambulance crested the hill. Mike flashed his lights and they pulled over. A man and a woman in blue EMT uniforms hopped out of the ambulance and yanked open the back doors. They pulled the stretcher out, then rolled it over beside Mike's truck.

Mike jumped out and briefed the EMT's. "She's breathing, and her pulse is faint. She hit her head pretty hard, and I had to cut her out of her seat belt and pull her out before the car went up in flames. You'll need to protect her neck. I don't have any idea how bad the injuries are."

Mike ran around the truck, opened the other door and helped them get her out after they put the neck brace on and slid a back board under her. He walked behind them, watching them put her in the ambulance.

"Dr. Mike, do you know her? She doesn't look like anyone from around here," the female EMT said. She was already jumping inside the back of the ambulance and starting to hook the injured woman up to the monitoring equipment.

"Nope, I have no idea."

She started to close the door.

Mike grabbed the handle. "Take good care of her. I'll follow you to the ER and come in to be with her."

The other medic shook his head. "We got this, you don't have to come."

But Mike couldn't go home until he made sure she'd be all right. "I'll meet you at the hospital."

When he arrived at the hospital, Mike didn't know what to do about the little dog. He coaxed it to eat some beef jerky, then left it in the car, setting a reminder on his phone to come out and check on him in an hour.

He wasn't licensed to practice in Montana, but he was going to advocate for her since she couldn't do it for herself. He did know something about trauma, and he would make sure she got the best care.

He strode into the ER and asked for her room. The nurses led him back to her cubicle, and as he walked in, his heart almost stopped at her beauty. She was lying in the bed, hooked up to an oxygen monitor, EKG, and heart rate monitor. Her head turned toward him as he entered. Her eyes fluttered open, and they were a gorgeous blue color, the color of the Caribbean Sea. With her dark brown hair and luscious lips, she was a knock-out. Mike walked to her bedside, pulled up a stool, and grasped her hand. Her eyes had closed again, and Mike looked up at the monitors. Everything was reading normal, and the huge weight on his chest lightened a little.

The ER doctor came in. "Are you her family?"

"No, I found her and pulled her out of the wreckage. I don't know who her family is, so I'm going to stay here with her until she wakes up."

"Ok, we have her scheduled for a CAT scan in the next couple of hours and x-ray should be in here shortly to check for rib and pelvic fractures. We have to clean up her cuts, and I have a plastic surgeon coming in to do her stitches, but he won't be here until the morning. We'll give her antibiotics to cover once everything else is clear. I'm working on getting a room for her in the meantime."

"Thanks, that sounds like a good plan."

A short while later, she was moved to her room, and Mike left to find a place to board the dog while she got her CAT scan.

When Mike returned, the urge to touch her almost overwhelmed him, and he felt even more determination to see her through this injury. A nurse walked in as he stood over her bed, looking closely at her cuts and bandages.

"Dr. Mike, do you know her? We have her down as Jane Doe, but if you—"

"I have no idea who she is. I just found her at the scene, and I want to make sure she's ok. Can you get me a recliner to sleep in?"

The nurse looked at him quizzically. "Sure," she muttered as she left the room.

The doctor entered later. "We found no internal bleeding, but she does have a very mild concussion. Airbags kept her from getting a fracture, and her neck is fine, just going to be sore for a few days. The plastic surgeon will sew up her forehead in the morning, but for now it's a butterfly closure. It's not our normal practice to let people stay overnight in the rooms, but I'll make an exception for you tonight. They're bringing you a chair."

The hospital noises were nothing Mike hadn't gotten used to as a trauma doctor in Seattle over the last ten years, and he found it easy to drift into sleep as he lay in the recliner. His thoughts wandered back to the night he hadn't been able to save another woman in his life. Memories haunted him, and kept him from sleeping. *This time will be different.*

Around 9:00 pm, Sheriff John Williams arrived at the hospital. "Dr. Mike, I figured you were here. How is she doing?"

"She's actually doing really well. All the signs point to a good outcome," Mike said with a smile on his face.

"And how are *you* doing?" the sheriff asked pointedly. "I know this can't be easy, and I'm wondering why you're here. She's not a local, probably just headed to Yellowstone for the weekend."

The silence in the room was palpable, and Mike looked down at his hands. "I couldn't leave her there, and I can't leave her here alone with no one. It's what I would have wanted for my wife in the same situation. But it's not the same thing that happened before. She's not going to die."

Over the last few months, Sheriff John and Mike had talked about what brought him back to Montana. He'd grown up here but had left for college in Washington State and ended up living in Seattle. Mike didn't really need to be reminded of how close this situation was to his own past.

"Okay, Doc, I didn't mean to ruffle your feathers. I checked out the accident scene, and she's lucky you found her. I hope she can tell us what happened, because there is nothing identifiable about that car."

After the sheriff left, Mike whispered a prayer for her, with the understanding that he had no control over the outcome of this car accident, but that he had done what he could. He only hoped it was enough.

Chapter 2

As the night grew longer, Mike's vigil over the stranger continued. She slept; sometimes she kicked, moaned, and moved her arms. Mike remained in the chair, watching the monitors closely. He occasionally got up and walked over to the bed and looked at her. So what if it was unreasonable for him to be here? He had always let his medical knowledge blend with his gut feeling – and right now his gut said he needed to stay with her. His gut feeling was right 99% of the time.

Mike thought back to his early days as a doctor, when he was in medical school. The long hours and sleepless nights that he endured to learn how to be a healer had toughened him. He'd always wanted to help people. How many nights when he was a resident had he sat up worried about a patient in his care? He'd always worried he hadn't done the right thing or missed something important. And then, eight months ago, he had left it all behind to move back to this remote place and lick his wounds. How had his life gotten so overwhelming that he had left what he thought was his calling for the solitude of the mountains? For the first time, he began to wonder if he'd done the right thing. Maybe he'd hidden from the world long enough.

When he'd pulled this girl out of that car, he'd felt alive for the first time since he'd learned of his wife's death.

After a fitful night of sleeping off and on, Mike stood up and stretched. Her eyelids fluttered open, and he rushed to her bedside. Mike smiled at her and grasped her hand. Her mouth formed an "O" and she pulled back her hand and pushed down on the bed, as if trying to sit up.

"Don't try to move too quickly. You're safe, you're in a hospital, but you were in an accident, and we want to make sure you're ok." Mike backed away from the bed a little to keep her from trying to jump out and run away. He looked into her gorgeous blue eyes and realized she was scared but strong. Her lovely features showed resolve, and in the blink of an eye she gathered her composure and took in her surroundings. She bit her lip and shook her head. "Where am I?"

Mike pulled his chair over to the bedside. It was still early, about 6:00 am, and he didn't know where to start.

"You had a car accident, and I found you and pulled you from your car. The ambulance brought you to the nearest hospital to make sure you didn't have any serious injuries. Your car is apparently completely burned, but you appear to have very little damage. How do you feel?" Mike tried to speak slowly and evaluate her reaction.

She shook her head again, squinted at him, and pressed her lips together tightly. "Who are you? Do I know you?"

"No, I was going to ask you the same thing once we made sure you were ok." Mike smiled at her and tried to relax, but he was sitting on the edge of his chair and rubbing his hands on his jeans to keep from reaching for her hand again. "My name is Mike Becker. I'm a doctor."

"I can't seem to remember who I am. My mind is blank at the moment, and I have no idea what's going on." She looked at him as though he could provide the answers.

He ran his hand through his short dark blond hair and rubbed his slightly rough chin, then ran a finger over his bottom lip. "Well, that is a problem but not the biggest one right now. How do you feel?" He stood up and walked toward the head of the bed to look at her eyes a little closer.

"I feel ok," she said, rubbing her arms and reaching up to touch the cut over her eyebrow that was going to need stitches. "Do I have a lot of cuts? Anything broken?"

"They did a scan and everything looks fine, just a mild concussion. You were driving a nice car, so it probably saved you from a lot of damage. It caught fire as I was pulling you out, so we don't have your ID or anything." Mike reached over and moved her soft silky hair from her forehead. Much to his surprise, she didn't jump. "Are you thirsty? Hungry? I can get you some water."

"That would be nice." Her blue eyes locked with his and then she glanced down quickly at her hands.

After Mike left the room, she started racking her brain to figure out who she was. Just one little clue. *Please let me remember. I don't want to be lost.* The only anchor in her world right now was Mike. He'd been so sweet in the way he'd tried to calm her and the gentle way he brushed back her hair. His hands were warm, his voice reassuring. *It will be ok.*

Mike returned with a nurse and some water.

"The plastic surgeon is going to come by and stitch up your forehead this morning. They don't let the ER docs do that because people get mad about having a scar. And your doctor said you can get out of bed as soon as you can, to walk and see if you have any other neurological damage." The nurse was brusque in her tone and made her feel like she was a burden to her just being in the room.

Mike seemed to sense that because he walked over to her side and told the nurse, "I'll help her get out of bed and take a few laps of the hallway, whatever she can handle. She does seem to have some post-traumatic amnesia and cannot recall her name or other information."

"I'll tell the doctor." The nurse turned and left the room.

Mike smiled and handed her the water. "Don't be offended, she doesn't have the best bedside manners. For what it's worth, I'm really glad you're feeling good and are awake."

She sighed and took a sip of water. The plastic surgeon arrived, and Mike offered to hold her hand while the surgeon gave her some lidocane to numb the area before he did the stitches. Mike rubbed his other hand over her knuckles and winced when she bit her lip when the surgeon inserted the needle.

As quickly as the platic surgeon had stitched her up, he was gone, and the next doctor entered. The doctor in charge of her care walked in and stood by her bedside. "Well, young lady, it sounds like you're doing well. The nurse tells me you don't remember much and may have some amnesia?"

"I don't know my name or who I am right now, and I can't recall anything from before the accident." She looked at Mike for a moment to see if he was going to say anything. She felt almost like he should talk for her, but he said nothing. "Is that going to last forever? Will I ever remember who I am?"

"It's hard to say. Post-traumatic amnesia can be temporary or there may be parts of your life you'll never remember. It's something you can work on and sometimes it spontaneously returns. I need to do an exam to test your neurological responses." The doctor got out his stethoscope and started to listen to her heart.

Mike stood up to leave her alone with the doctor, but she reached out and grasped his hand. "You don't have to leave."

"I'll be back in a couple of minutes. I'm just going to let him do his work and stretch my legs. When I get back, we can take a stroll around the floor." Mike smiled at her, and her heart beat a little faster. He was very attractive, with dark brown eyes and blond hair, a shadow of beard on his strong jaw.

"Ok." She turned back to the doctor. "All right, tell me how I'm doing."

The doctor tested her reflexes by tapping on her knees, having her raise both eyebrows, frown, close her eyes tightly and try to open them, smiling and puffing out her cheeks. He also told her the results of her CAT scan from the day before.

She was relieved to find out she was doing fine, with no internal bleeding or broken bones. Just some stitches. She was not seriously injured, and might even be able to go "home" today if she could walk around without assistance and keep her food down. *But where is home?*

"Thanks," she told the doctor. "I'm going to get up, walk around, and get out of this room. But I don't know where I'll go if I leave the hospital."

Mike walked in and heard her saying that. "When you're ready to leave, I have a guest bedroom and you can stay at my house until you're well enough. I'll help you work on finding your family."

"But you barely even know me," she whispered, even though her heart was singing with the thought of spending more time with him.

"It's not a problem. I have plenty of room. Not only do I not mind, I *want* you to come to my house and stay until you feel better." Mike walked over to the bedside. "Please."

The doctor looked between them. "We can find a shelter for you to stay in if you don't want to go to his house, but I can vouch for his reputation as an honorable person in this community. You would be safe there."

"Okay, okay, I'll think about it. But for now, let me see if I can walk around here first or I may not have to worry about it." She laughed.

"I'll be back in a couple of hours to check on you and see how you're doing and make a decision about what to do next," the doctor said to both of them.

As he left, Mike sat down and rubbed his hands together. "I didn't mean to make you uncomfortable by offering my house, but I would be glad to let you stay there and do what

I can to help. I was an ER doctor. I'm not currently practicing medicine but I have the ability to help you if you have a problem."

She felt the genuineness in his voice, but sensed something else that he was not talking about. Nothing bad, just holding back something. Clearly he could take care of her. She wasn't afraid of him, and she wasn't sure she liked the other choice of going to a shelter.

"Ok, should we get up and take a walk?" she asked.

Mike seemed relieved to change the subject. "Sure, let me get the nurse to unhook you from the machines." He left and returned quickly with the nurse from earlier. The nurse gave her another gown to put around her so nothing would be exposed, and then made quick work of getting her untangled and helping her to stand. Mike moved quickly to her other side, grasped the IV pole with one hand and put his other arm around her waist to steady her.

The nurse released her and she shifted her weight to Mike as she let her legs adjust to standing. Now that she was moving around, she felt sore all over. Like a big bruise. Mike led her around the end of the bed and toward the door, pulling the IV pole beside them. Once they were outside the room, Mike loosened his grip on her waist and let her stand in one place to get her bearings. She took one tentative step forward, then another, until she was walking slowly around the nursing unit. "This feels great, even if I am a little sore."

He smiled and nodded his head, paying close attention to her walking and how steady she was. "You're doing well. I am going to loosen my hold and let you walk by yourself a bit but I'll be right here behind you." Mike let her go, and she hesitated a little, then started going forward again.

"Come walk beside me, I don't want to have to yell at you behind me. Plus, I can't imagine what the view is back there," she said with a laugh. So he walked beside her with his hand gently at the small of her back as they toured the rest of the unit's six beds, three of which were empty.

While they were walking, she decided to quiz him about being a doctor. "Why are you no longer practicing as a doctor? What made you stop?"

Mike sighed. "I don't know if you ever stop being a doctor, but my wife died in a car accident a year ago, and I no longer felt I could practice at my best. People deserve you at your best, especially in the ER, so I left and moved here, where I grew up, and bought a ranch – without any cattle – and have lived here for the last eight months."

"Oh, sorry." She cringed at the thought of bringing up his wife's death. It had obviously been a traumatic event for him, since he'd stopped practicing medicine.

"Don't feel bad. I need to start living in the real world again instead of hiding out. I actually have some of her clothes at the house I haven't gotten rid of and you're about her size. I can bring some over for you to wear out of the hospital if you like. That is, if you're planning on coming to stay at my house now that you know my deepest darkest secret?" Mike grinned and waited for her to answer.

"That sounds fine. I can come and stay at your house, if you're sure you won't mind," she said.

"Oh, I forgot that you have a dog! Do you remember your dog, perhaps? I put him in a kennel last night, when you were getting your

CAT scan, but we have to go get him when you leave the hospital," Mike told her.

"No, I don't remember, but a dog sounds like something that I might like. How did you find him?" she asked.

"He ran behind me when I pulled you from the car and jumped into the truck with us, so I figured he was yours. We can get him later." They were standing in the middle of the hall talking, not walking, and the nurses were watching them, so Mike gave her a rueful grin. "Let's head back to your room and talk some more, out of the spotlight." He gestured toward the nurse's station, and she understood what he was saying. She nodded and they turned and went back to her room.

Her breakfast of hot soup and coffee had arrived. She sipped the soup and drank water. She didn't need any help with eating, and her stomach was not hurting either.

"I'm going to go back to my house and gather some clothing for you and make sure the guest room is ready. I'll be back in a couple of hours, ok?" He grasped her hand and squeezed it. She nodded ok, and he turned to go. She watched him leave, feeling a bit lost once he was gone. Right now, she had no one else.

28 | Page

Chapter 3

When Mike got to his log cabin, he brought in the groceries that were still ok and threw out the rest. He would need to go to the grocery store again before she came over so he would have food to feed them. He was not sure if she would be released today or tomorrow, but he already could see she wasn't going to have to stay long.

He went into the guest room and changed the sheets and rearranged some furniture so she would have an easy time moving around. He had purchased the house fully furnished and did not spend much time in the room, so he cleaned it up as quickly as he could. He didn't want to leave her at the hospital alone for too long. He felt a strong desire to be there to comfort her. He didn't have much experience with amnesia, since most of the patients he saw in the ER with brain injuries were unconscious. He held out hope that her memory would come back quickly, so she could get back to her family. He knew how it felt to lose someone precious.

After cleaning the guest room, he strode up the staircase to his own room and walked into the closet. He pulled out the boxes in the back containing Jocelyn's clothing. The clothing still smelled like her perfume, and he couldn't bear letting go of them when he moved. He grabbed a plain pink T-shirt and jeans that had rhinestones on them, and then added underwear, shoes, and socks to the pile. He was surprised he didn't feel the same longing for Jocelyn that had been there just a few months ago when he opened the boxes. It had been a year, and this morning was the first time he'd told someone about her without the lump in his throat.

He took a quick shower, shaved, and changed his clothes. He put on a red and white flannel shirt and blue jeans. As he pulled on his boots, he smiled and thought about how the last 24 hours had turned into a blessing instead of another tragedy. He got into his truck and headed back to the hospital with the clothes.

When he made it back to her room, she was sitting up talking to another doctor, and he waited outside her door for them to finish. As the doctor got up to leave, she waved Mike in with a big smile on her face. "They said I can leave today, since you're a doctor. I don't have to stay another night! Maybe I can get some real food at your house instead of soup." She was almost hopping out of bed with excitement.

"That's great news. I'll be glad to make whatever you want to eat." Mike was so caught up in the moment he walked over to the bed and hugged her. Then he realized what he was doing and quickly stepped back. She had hugged him back, so he didn't feel like he was overstepping a boundary, but he was suddenly aware that he needed to be careful to not get too caught up in her because she did have a home to go back to.

"When are you going to be able to leave?" Mike asked.

"They said after lunch. I have to walk around some more – I did a couple of laps after you left – and I should be out of here by two. It's almost noon now, so not too much longer. What did you bring me to wear?" She reached for the bag.

"Some jeans and a shirt and other stuff," he said. "I hope it will fit."

"I'll try it on, and if it doesn't, the nurse said I could have some scrubs to wear back to your house till I can get something that fits," she said.

Just then, the admissions department woman came in. "Ma'am, we need to enter your insurance information into the computer for billing purposes."

"Oh, I don't have any information. I lost it all in the car fire. I don't even remember my name. Are you going to let me leave?" she asked, sounding a little panicked.

"I can pay the bill," Mike offered. "Once we find out who she is, she can file with her insurance company. You can put me on the bill as the person responsible."

She put her hand on his arm and shook her head. "It will be a lot of money. I don't want you to do that."

"It's ok, I can handle it, and you can pay me back. No worries, it will be fine," Mike said, then proceeded to give the admissions lady his name and address. She charged him a $500 deposit and left the room.

"You shouldn't have done that," she said, sounding a little upset.

"I bet that before the bill even comes, you have your memory back and you'll be able to take care of it," Mike said with a smile. "Don't worry about it, worry about getting better."

"Ok," she said. He couldn't tell if she was still upset that he said he would pay or just being thoughtful.

She brightened up when her lunch came; they brought her a chicken noodle soup and a turkey sandwich. She ate everything and said she didn't feel sick to her stomach at all. Mike was relieved. He wanted to leave as much as she did.

"Okay, I'm going to get up and walk around this unit so we can leave," she said, getting out of bed on her own.

Mike rushed over to her side when he realized she was moving, but she didn't need any help. "Want me to walk beside you?"

"As long as you don't try to help me. I have to do this myself if we are going to leave," she quipped. He laughed and put his hands in the air as if to say, "hands off!" and walked out behind her until they were at a spot in the hall where he could walk beside her.

"How's the dog doing?" she asked.

"I don't know, we'll go get him on the way back to the house. I didn't want to stop by there before I got back to the hospital," he told her.

"Well, I want to meet this little hero! He sounds like a loyal friend," she said.

"He certainly didn't want to leave your side, and didn't like going to the kennel, but I didn't have a choice since I wanted to stay with you to make sure you were ok," Mike told her.

She turned and looked at him. "You stayed here all night, in my room? Why?"

"It's a bit of a story, but mainly because I didn't want you to wake up and be alone. I wanted you to know someone cared, even if it's a stranger," he said.

"Oh, thank you. Perhaps you'll tell me the whole story later." She turned to go back toward her room. She was walking just fine, with no residual effect from the mild concussion. Mike thought that boded well for her memory return.

Once the doctor returned, the hospital released her into Mike's care. He was not at all worried about taking care of her, but he was worried about the fact that he had grown so attached to her in the last 24 hours. He had already told her more about his life than anyone in this town knew, including the sheriff. What made him feel so comfortable around her?

She, on the other hand, was terribly nervous about going to Mike's house. It wasn't so much that she didn't know him, because she felt safe with him and knowing he was an experienced doctor made her feel at ease. She felt calm and relaxed around him, and loved the way he held her hand and anticipated her needs. She liked the way he cared for her, but that made her nervous, because she had no idea if she had someone else waiting wherever she came from. If her feelings for Mike became too strong, they were bound to complicate her life in ways she didn't even know yet.

They drove to the kennel, and she could tell the little dog knew her well. He wriggled all over and jumped straight up and down at her feet. She couldn't help but pick him up and snuggle him while he licked her face.

"Do you recognize the dog? Does he ring a bell?" Mike asked.

She thought for a moment, but shook her head. "No, he doesn't, but he obviously recognizes me." She smiled at how much the dog was trying to lick her hands. She was petting him but he couldn't get enough of her attention.

After Mike paid the kennel, they drove to the local grocery store. Mike told her she could stay in the car if she didn't feel like walking around, but she decided to go in. She felt shaky at first, not as confident as she had been in the hospital, but she felt determined to stand up and walk through the store. She might be tired later, but she wanted to prove to herself that she was strong enough to do this. The grocery store trip was quick, and Mike picked up dog food and a few other things.

She could sense that he was walking closely behind her by the way he almost put his hand on her back to make sure she was steady when they walked down an aisle, but she had the grocery cart to hold her up and she was steadfast in her ability to show she was ok. She hated feeling weak.

Once they were in the car and the groceries were loaded, she let out a big sigh. Mike smiled. "I thought you were tired in there. Why didn't you stay in the car and rest? You'll have enough time to push yourself later."

"I can't stand to just sit here. It's why I was glad to leave the hospital. They made me feel so needy," she told him.

"Perhaps because you *are* needy. You were in a traumatic accident, you know. You need to be careful." He gently grasped her chin to turn her face toward him. "I need you to go slow and let yourself heal. If you push yourself after a head injury, you could have more problems. Listen to what your body is telling you, ok?" His face was so close to hers, and she felt goose bumps on her skin as she looked into his brown eyes. His expression softened after the quick reprimand, and he smiled at her.

"All right," she murmured. "I promise I'll go slow."

On the way to his house, he turned on the radio, and she leaned her head back to close her eyes and listen. The music floated around in her head, and she started humming some tunes.

She woke as she heard the bell in the truck ding when Mike opened his door. He rushed around to her side. "Let's get you inside and settled in." He turned so she could put her hand on his shoulder as she stepped out of the truck.

Mike placed his arm around her waist and supported her gently. She felt the warmth of his hand through her T-shirt and relaxed a little. Once she was standing on solid ground, she turned to Mike and grinned. "Ok, I'm ready to go. Can you carry the dog?"

"Sure." He let go of her and picked up the little one and followed behind her as she walked along the bumpy path toward the house. He caught up to her as she reached the door and slid past her to open it. "Your room is over here." He swept his arm to the right, and she followed him into what must be his guest room. "Please sit down and relax. You've had a long day, and it's almost time for supper."

She nodded and sat down in a rocking chair. Mike put the little dog down and excused himself to get the groceries out of the car, shutting the door as he left. She let out a huge sigh and let her head fall back. *It's going to be ok, it's going to be ok.* The dog jumped up on her lap, making a couple of turns and then laying down. She patted his head and looked around the room. Her bed was covered with a colorful quilt, and she had a bedside table with a lamp. The only other furniture was the rocking chair she was sitting in. A wool area rug covered most of the floor. She stood up and walked to the window and looked out. She could see Mike carrying groceries from the truck into the house, and a large front yard with a winding drive. She couldn't see the road from her window, but the view was spectacular. The mountains rose up in front of her with their white caps, and evergreen trees dotted the landscape.

Tears pricked her eyes, and she wondered why she suddenly felt like crying. Was it the sadness of the accident, even though she had lived through it, or the sudden realization of what was happening? She was here in a house in the middle of Montana with a nice, handsome stranger who anticipated her needs and whose kindness made her stomach go flip-flop every time he smiled at her or touched her, but somewhere out there, someone was wondering about her and worried about her. Did Mike know what he did to her? She wasn't sure.

Mike saw her standing in the window, looking out with the dog in her arms. She had survived a serious accident and her physical recovery seemed to be on track, but the amnesia would be another story. She was a beautiful woman, and he couldn't imagine she was single, so he reminded himself to tread carefully. He loved the way she was so kind and sweet, with an innocence that wasn't contrived, unlike most of the women he had known in his life, except for Jocelyn. He wondered what Jocelyn would think of his life now and how he had hidden himself from the outside world.

Shaking his head a little to clear his thoughts, he brought the last of the groceries in and started putting them away in the kitchen.

She came out of her room and sat on a barstool. The kitchen was an open area, with plenty of cabinet space, granite countertops, and stainless steel appliances. Pots and pans hung invitingly over the stove. Warmth exuded from the space and made her feel comfortable.

"I would offer to help, but I know you won't let me. What can I do?"

"You're right, young lady," Mike told her. "I'll put the groceries away and make us some dinner. Do you want something hot or cold?"

"A sandwich sounds really good, actually," she said. "Are you sure I'm not going to be a problem for you?"

Mike sensed her true feelings in that sentence. She was lost and wanted reassurance. "You're absolutely not a burden. I'm living here alone, and I welcome your company. I'm already looking forward to our dinner conversation." He grinned at her and winked.

She let out a sigh of relief. "Ok, but tell me if I get to be too much."

"Not going to happen. How about a turkey and cheese sandwich?" Mike started to gather the food together to make their supper. He got her a glass of ice water, then washed his hands and set two plates on the counter, added the bread, cheese, turkey and mayonnaise, then cut them diagonally. Putting a handful of chips on each plate, he slid hers over to her, filled his own glass with water, and came to sit beside her.

"After dinner, I'll show you around the house. You can go anywhere in the house or in the yard, but let me know if you're going to go outside so I can check on you. I don't want you to fall down. The ground is a little uneven, and you're still regaining your footing," Mike told her. "We can go for a walk in the morning to explore the woods around us, and I can show you my jogging trails. The mountains are breathtaking."

"I would like that. I'm feeling a little overwhelmed right now, and my mind is going a mile a minute. A walk would be good. The room is great, I really appreciate it. I can't say that enough. I don't know what I can do to repay you," she said.

Mike shook his head. He reached over and put his hand over hers. "Don't worry about that right now. Focus on your recovery, please. I'm here to take care of you."

She swallowed and shook her head. They finished the meal in silence.

After he cleaned up the plates, he leaned over the counter toward her. "Do you still feel like a tour of the house?"

"I feel much better now that I've had a good meal. That was great. Let's go." She slid off her chair and came around the counter to stand beside him.

"Well, you've seen the kitchen. Eat anything you like. We can go back to the grocery store whenever you like." Mike guided her out of the kitchen to the stairs. He walked beside her to make sure she got her bearings. At the top of the stairs, he led her to his room.

"Here is my room." His room was furnished with a huge king-sized wooden four-poster bed. He had a couple of rocking chairs and a couch, and his computer sat on a desk, next to a picture of a beautiful woman.

"Is this your wife?" she asked as she picked up the picture.

"Yes, that's Jocelyn." Mike hoped she got the message loud and clear that he didn't want to talk about it right now.

He opened his closet doors. "In the back are the boxes where I got some clothes for you earlier today. I'll bring them downstairs later and you can choose anything you feel like wearing. Let's go see the rest of the house."

They walked down the large staircase, with its roughhewn railing and a soft carpet runner. The house had a very warm feeling, with all the brown and beige in the decor. When they reached the bottom, they stood in the great room with the large front entranceway, and a large sitting area—couch and fireplace with lots of wood ready to go for any cold night. She looked around in amazement at the high ceilings and wooden walls. An area rug in the middle of the sitting room was colorful with reds, browns, and oranges. The couches were oversized, in brown leather. Lamps stood in the corners to light the area, and a coffee table with large photo books sat in the center.

Finally, they got back to the spare room where she had been staying. He showed her the bathroom and reminded her she should be very careful with washing her face because of the stitches. She sat down on the bed, and the little dog, who had been following them around the entire house, hopped up onto the bed and snuggled in beside her. She put her hand on the little Yorkie and bent down to kiss his head. "Oh, I guess we should feed him something! I think we bought some dog food, right?"

"Yep, I forgot about him too, but at least we remembered to buy him food. We can take him to the kitchen and fix him a bowl. It's been a long day, and you seem kind of tired, so maybe we should think about getting to bed after that. I can get the clothes from upstairs and if you want to find a book to read you can get something from the library next to my room." Mike picked up the dog as he headed toward the kitchen.

Chapter 4

After the dog ate, they walked outside together to let him go to the bathroom. They sat on the back porch swing and watched the sun set over the mountains as the sounds of birds and insects rang through the air. She laid her head on his shoulder and closed her eyes, and within a few deep breaths she was asleep. He put his arm around her and sat with her for a moment, just listening to her breathe, wanting to take her to his room and hold her close so he could watch over her instead of leaving her alone in the guest room.

He rose and picked her up, carrying her inside with the dog trailing behind. He sat her in the chair, and she awakened a little.

"Oh, I fell asleep. I'm sorry. I guess I am tired." She rubbed her eyes.

He walked toward the bed and pulled back the covers. She was still groggy, and had unbuttoned her jeans and started to pull them off. He had to look up at the ceiling to keep from staring, and his cock immediately responded. He continued to look at the ceiling as she finished getting the jeans off and stumbled over to the bed and crawled in under the covers.

"Good night," she mumbled, and patted the bed. The little dog seemed to think that was his cue, and he jumped up and crawled under the covers to snuggle up beside her. Mike reached over and smoothed her hair, pulled the covers up around her. She was already asleep.

Mike walked up the stairs to his room, undressed in the bathroom, and turned on the shower. His cock was hard as a rock, and the woman downstairs was responsible. In the shower, he poured some shower gel in his hand. He grasped his hard-on and stroked the length, going slowly and thinking about having her in his arms. He closed his eyes and stroked faster, imagining her soft lips and sweet voice, dreaming of holding her breasts in his hands as he showered them with kisses. He was in a good rhythm now, and the pressure built as he imagined pulling down her panties and licking her wetness. He stroked faster as the orgasm came over him and his balls tightened with his ejaculation. He leaned his head against the wall and breathed heavily. Finishing his shower, he dried off and got into bed.

As he lay there trying to sleep, he reflected upon how much he'd closed himself off from the world, only talking to his brother occasionally and the people at the store when he went to town. He couldn't continue this self-imposed isolation, and he'd proven to himself that he was still able to care for a car wreck victim without it affecting him. He had gone on auto-pilot when he saw the car accident and hadn't thought about Jocelyn until after the immediate crisis had past. Tonight he'd realized how much he liked having another person around to talk to. He was not sure how long she would need to recover and if she would even ever remember her past, but he was glad she was here. Part of him wished he had the same problem.

* * *

In the morning, Mike brought down the rest of the clothes for her to sort through. He knocked on her door, and the little dog scratched at it in reply. "Hey, I'm going to crack the door a little and let the little guy out. I brought down the clothes, and I'll leave them sitting outside the door. If you still want to go for a walk, let me know."

"Ok," she replied sleepily.

The little dog ran out and raced to the back door. He jogged over and opened it, then walked to the swing and sat down. In a couple of minutes, the dog was done and they headed back into the house toward the guest room.

"We're back. Do you want to go for a walk?" He noticed she had pulled the boxes of clothing into the room.

"Yes," she told him. "I'll be ready in a minute."

"Ok, I'll wait for you in the kitchen."

When she walked in the kitchen a couple of minutes later, he was amazed. She had on some sweats and a short sleeved shirt, with her hair pulled back in a ponytail. Her blue eyes made his heart beat a little faster. The clothes were Jocelyn's, but the look was all her. Her skin glowed with a good night's rest, and she exuded energy. Her smile was contagious.

Mike stood up. "It appears you had a good night's sleep."

She laughed. "I slept so well I don't remember getting into bed."

Mike looked up at the ceiling. "I carried you to your room, and you got yourself into bed."

"Did you undress me?" she asked.

"Nope, you just took off your jeans and crawled into bed," he said, blushing.

"Oh." Now it was her turn to blush.

"Anyway, let's go for a walk. I have a good path figured out that won't be too difficult but is very pretty," Mike said, trying to change the subject. She nodded and followed him out the door.

They walked for about ten minutes, not really talking. Once they reached the clearing in the woods at the end of the path, Mike motioned to some rocks for them to sit on. She sat down and looked out at the mountains. Mike settled on the rock beside her and started pointing out the different peaks.

"Did I take off my clothes in front of you last night?" she asked.

Mike's eyebrows rose. "You just pulled off your jeans, and I swear I looked at the ceiling. You were so tired. You don't have to be embarrassed. I understand."

"Wow, I am not sure what to say."

"Once again, you don't have to worry about it. I have seen women in panties before. Can we forget about it?" Mike asked. "Are you feeling out of breath? We are at a higher elevation here than you're probably used to, and it can make it hard to breathe."

"I am a little out of breath. My legs are fine though. I'm just trying to catch my breath a little and then we can head back."

Mike wanted to tell her it would all be ok, and that she was going to recover from this and go back to her life, but he wasn't sure he wanted her to leave so quickly. Once she was gone, he would be back to his regular routine, and that seemed like a sad prospect right now. But he didn't say anything, and they walked back to the house quietly.

"Come on into the kitchen, and I'll make you some breakfast," Mike said as they walked into the house.

She nodded and sat at the bar. It had only been two days since the accident, and she was very fortunate to have almost no physical damage, save the little stitches on her forehead. She watched as Mike walked around the kitchen and gathered the items for breakfast. First, he pulled out the milk and sat it on the counter. Then the bowls and spoons for cereal, then the cereal itself. Finally some orange juice and glasses.

He had a rhythmic way of moving, and she could almost see a list in his head that he was checking off as he worked.

She thought back to the night before and did not recall getting undressed and crawling into bed. She remembered them walking to the back porch and sitting down, but after that she must have fallen asleep. Her cheeks heated with embarrassment as she thought of what she did, and how he'd reacted. *He's a gentleman.* No use in worrying over it, though. She needed to do some research in the medical books he had upstairs about post-traumatic amnesia.

Mike sat the bowl of cereal in front of her, and she looked up at him and smiled. He glanced from her eyes to her mouth, then quickly away. "Is something wrong?" she asked.

"No, you just look lost in thought. What were you thinking about?"

"I was thinking about doing research on head injuries and post-traumatic amnesia today by reading some of the books in the library."

He walked around the counter and sat next to her at the bar. She turned to him. "You're really my hero, and I'm so thankful that you—a doctor—found me."

Mike bowed his blond head and said quietly, "I wouldn't have left you."

She reached over and touched his hand, and he looked up into her eyes again. She smiled. "I feel like it was fate that you found me."

He pressed his lips together, as if to keep from saying something. "You're welcome," Mike said at last. "We'll find your past again, don't worry."

With that, they both started to eat and quiet settled over them again. They cleaned up the kitchen together after they ate, and then went their separate ways to get ready for the day.

After Mike showered and dressed, the doorbell rang. When he answered it, he found the sheriff had stopped by to check up on Mike's houseguest. Mike led him to the living room.

"Any news about the accident victim?" the sheriff asked as he took a chair.

"She has amnesia, and I'm not sure how long it will be before she starts to remember. I'm fine with her being here, more than fine; she can stay as long as she needs," Mike said.

The sheriff laughed. "Don't mind how long she stays, huh? That sounds real neighborly, Mike. How is she doing otherwise?"

"She's doing remarkably well. Not many people come home the day after an accident like that. I shudder to think about what would have happened if I hadn't come upon her…" Mike trailed off, thinking of her trapped in that car when it caught fire.

The sheriff patted him on the shoulder. "Whether you like it or not, you were the right person to find her. You saved her life."

With that, they looked up and saw her standing in the doorway, watching them talk. Mike jumped up and went over to her to see if she was ok. She walked to the couch and sat down to face the sheriff.

"Hello, I should formally introduce myself. I'm Sheriff John Williams. I'm the lawman around Big Sky, and I was talking to Mike about what happened in your accident a couple of days ago. Can you tell me what you remember about it?" the sheriff asked her.

"Honestly, it's just a blank. I can't remember anything before I woke up yesterday morning. I keep hoping it will come flooding back, and I can call my family and let them know I'm ok, but so far, nothing." She let out a big sigh.

Mike walked over and sat beside her, putting his arm around her shoulders. "It's going to come back, just give it some time. Sheriff has some news about the accident."

"Your car was burned beyond recognition. Nothing was recovered, except for a partial VIN number on the frame. We're trying to run it and find out who owned the car, but we have limited resources, so it will take a bit of time," Sheriff John told her. "What's left of your car is at the local tow shop."

"Oh, so if you can find out who is the owner of the car, you can probably find out who I am, great! How long will that take?" she asked.

"It might take a couple of weeks. But I also want to take your fingerprints to run through the state crime lab and see if we get a match." The sheriff got out his kit to take her prints. "Don't get your hopes up. You're probably not in the system. And the state may take a few weeks to run the prints anyway. It's all I can do for you now to help figure out the mystery." He got up to leave.

"Thanks, John." Mike stood and shook his hand. "I'm sure you're doing your best. Thanks for taking the time to come out here personally. I'll keep you informed about any new breakthroughs."

The sheriff tipped his hat to Mike and left.

* * *

"What would you like to eat?" Mike asked later that evening. They had only eaten cereal and sandwiches so far, and he wanted to make something more filling.

"I'm not sure. You can make me whatever, and as long as it smells good I'll eat it! I'm getting pretty hungry after all that napping I did today." She laughed.

It was normal for her to need to rest, but he worried about what she felt now that the sheriff had come and gone with little help.

He made them chicken breasts on the grill, and jasmine rice and fresh green beans from the garden. He wondered what kind of thoughts were running through her head. He poured her a glass of water and himself a glass of wine. Once the meal was ready, he motioned for her to come in and sit down at the comfortable kitchen table. They dined as they watched the sun go down through the back window.

Mike relaxed a little because she was showing all the signs of physically recovering, and she was past the point of too much worry regarding her external wounds. Now, the hard part of finding out who she was would begin.

Once they finished the meal, they walked into the main living area and settled down in front of the fire.

"Tell me about my accident," she said, while he piled logs onto the fire for some warmth.

"Well, I was coming home from my grocery trip, and I saw your car on the side of the road. It had hit a pole, and all the airbags had deployed. Your head was lying against the side window, which I guess is how you got that gash on your forehead. The doors wouldn't open, so I had to smash in the window with my boot. Then I grabbed you out of the car, gingerly, because I was not sure how much you were hurt. As I ran, carrying you, your car burst into flames. The little dog joined us at the car."

"So, I was unconscious when you got there? How did I get to the hospital?" She had scrunched her eyebrows together, really trying to imagine the scene.

"I put you in my truck and called an ambulance to meet me. It's about a 50 minute drive to the hospital," Mike told her.

"Wow, I am seriously lucky you came along. I'm still curious why you're here in the middle of nowhere and not working as a doctor anymore," she said, asking the question that had been in her head all day. She got up, walked around, and looked at the pictures that were placed on the tables around the room.

Once the fire was started, he got up and sat in the oversized chair, and she sat down on the end of the couch nearest him. He rubbed his hands together. "I moved here to to re-examine what I wanted to do with the rest of my life. I was out of the country in Haiti on a mission trip when Jocelyn died. She suffered and died alone. I didn't even know about the accident for four days, and by then it was too late. I know she would have died from her injuries anyway, but I couldn't be there with her and comfort her."

Mike looked away from her, at the pictures around the room. "It was hard to manage being in our house without her after being married for five years. So I bought this house and moved here, back to the country life that I grew up in and away from being a doctor, because if I hadn't been away, I could have been there for here and she might not even have had the accident. My brother, Chris, flew out as soon as they called him, but he was too late." Tears started to form in the corners of his eyes as he remembered what he had lost and how angry he had been at the world for taking it away from him. He paused and pulled a handkerchief out of his pocket and dabbed his eyes.

She reached over and patted his hand. "I'm so sorry, Mike." She felt like she was invading his space and making him rip his wound right back open.

"We met in college. Jocelyn was going to nursing school, and I was in medical school. I loved Jocelyn from the moment I met her, and decided on our first date that I would marry her. Of course, I didn't tell her that. After we had dated for about six months, I proposed, and we went to Las Vegas and got married. We always planned to have children, but had not gotten around to it. Our lives were busy, and Jocelyn took on the life of a doctor's wife, doing a lot of charity work and being out and about…"

Mike's voice trailed off and then he looked at her.

She was watching him quietly, just listening, twirling a piece of hair in a nervous gesture. She wanted to reach over and touch him, to make him feel better, to let him know that she understood now why he was so intent on staying with her, and that on some level she hoped she wasn't just a way to assuage his pain over not being there when Jocelyn died.

"So that is why you have her clothes upstairs and the pictures around the house?" She reached over to touch a picture sitting near her.

"Yes, I could not bear to let them go. I know she's not coming back, but I have been in a holding pattern because I feel so guilty about what happened, even if it wasn't my fault," he said, staring at the fire.

He turned on the radio to a local music station, and some country music came out of the speakers. They sat there in silence for a couple of minutes.

Then he said, "You can wear whatever you want from that closet. I don't need to keep it. And you need it. "

"Thanks," she murmured and leaned back on the comfy leather and closed her eyes. She started humming the song, relaxing in the way the song sounded and feeling like she knew it.

It had only been a couple of days, but she still felt so very lost. Only with the music playing, which she just *felt* inside her, did she start to relax a little. Her thoughts turned to the man in the room with her. He was cute, with his luscious lips that frowned way too much and his strong, sturdy hands. He wore a flannel shirt and jeans with boots. She tried to not let her mind go down the path of seeing him without a shirt, but it was hard to do. So she kept closing her eyes and pretending to be into the music to keep from staring at him all night.

She sensed that he was attracted to her, from the way he had sat near her and touched her hand to soothe her earlier in the day, and the way he had looked at her eyes and then her lips at breakfast. Her body reacted to him as well as her mind, and she bit her lip to keep from getting up and kissing him to make him feel better.

"Are you ready for bed?" he asked. "You can come up to the library and get another book if you like."

She thought it might be nice to have a fiction book to read, since the scientific ones were sure to give her nightmares. They went upstairs to the library next to his room.

"It helps me go to sleep when I read before bed," he told her.

She chose a romance, and they walked downstairs so he could make sure the house was secure and the fire was out. She didn't mind him taking such good care of her and looked forward to spending time with him tomorrow, even if it was just to sit and read.

She went to her room, turned on the lamp, and started reading until she was ready to go to sleep. While she was reading, her dog jumped up on the bed and worked his head under her hand, signaling her that he wanted her to pet him. So she stroked his hair and scratched his belly for a little while, and then he crawled under the covers and curled up next to her as she was turning out the light to go to sleep. She laid in bed and tears slipped from the corners of her eyes. She wanted to scream out with frustration and fear. *At least I have a bed to sleep in. I could have been dead.*

* * *

Mike went to his room and sat in his chair for a long time reading, but not really seeing the pages. Talking about Jocelyn had stirred up the sorrow of her death and the wish that he'd had more time with her. He saw death every day when he worked in the emergency room, yet he didn't think it would be Jocelyn. She was always there for him when he needed her, and he could almost hear her voice telling him it was fine to start living again. She'd want that, not for him to be stuck in the middle of Montana with his grief. He had left his job because he could not cope with the pain and suffering of his patients anymore in combination with his own. It was normal for an ER doctor to burn out, but it was Jocelyn's sudden death he'd needed to deal with if he was being honest with himself, and the guilt he felt for leaving her, even if it was to help orphans in another country.

Maybe the accident and the girl were part of that moving on. He needed to take care of her until her memory returned or her family found her. He crawled into his bed for a night of tossing and turning and nightmares about seeing his wife's face intertwined with the woman he had just rescued.

Chapter 5

As she lay awake in her room downstairs the next morning, Mike got up and left the house, probably for a run. She rubbed her arms and felt the scrapes all up and down her skin from the accident. She looked up at the ceiling and tried to force her brain to let her past out, but it wasn't working. She was glad he was letting her stay here. Last night, when they had sat by the fire and she had listened to his story about his wife and the accident, she thought he was still dealing with a lot of grief, even just telling the story.

She wasn't sure if she had a family at home, but she wasn't wearing a ring. The only family she knew about was right here in bed with her, snuggled to her side, and she didn't even know his name. She should give him one, something that showed how daring and ferocious he really was. "Ok, from now on your name will be Brutus." He looked up at her, then snuggled his head back down. Apparently, that was ok with him. She picked him up and gave him a kiss on his head.

She had a book to read, but she couldn't concentrate on even one word of it. She was determined to figure out what the amnesia was and how to recover from it. She felt like she had a purpose in her life, and if she was driving a Lexus, she must have enough to get by. She hated having Mike paying for everything. It had irritated her in the hospital when he paid the deposit for the room, but she was trying to get her bearings and didn't want to be rude. *I can figure this out, no matter how long it takes.*

Her mind drifted to the man who was her caretaker for the moment, and even though the sun had just come up, she wondered what it would be like to have him hold her and adore her, lavishing kisses and caresses all over her body. She felt utterly dependent on him for her life, but her appreciation went beyond mere thanks. She wanted to thank him for saving her life by showing him in ways her mind was imagining. She didn't want to be dependent on him for his hospitality. She wanted to be a partner and let them heal each other's wounds. She wasn't sure that would be ok with Mike, but she was pretty sure she could convince him.

* * *

Mike routinely went for a run in the morning, and even though he worried about leaving her in the house alone, he needed the release that running gave him, much like the adrenaline rush that accompanied a night in the ER, except it didn't leave him worn out the next day. He loved this part of Montana, with the gorgeous mountains and secluded trails in the trees that led to even more spectacular views of the wilderness. He ran to his usual spot and stood looking out at the view. This silence and natural beauty was the thing that drew him here when the world was collapsing around him. He thought about Jocelyn, and how she never wanted to come back to the country after they were married. For her, a vacation was not really a vacation unless it involved expensive shopping and exotic locations. Mike had loved taking her places, but he grew up here in Montana with his brother Chris, and Montana renewed his soul. When he had needed peace, he'd known he would find it here.

Mike had gone a different direction than his brother. Mike became a doctor like his father, while Chris went to work for the FBI after college in their cybercrimes unit. He was an excellent computer programmer and even better stalker. He knew how to hunt down people who were very good at not leaving a trace, and Chris was one of the best at finding out where they were. If she didn't start to remember much soon, he would call his brother and see if he could lend a hand with tracking down her past. Chris had more options than the sheriff, Mike suspected, even when it came to fingerprints, and could probably help her find out more about her past than she ever wanted to know.

She was in the kitchen singing when he returned from his run. He listened to her voice, and realized she had a fantastic quality that sounded like she did it on a regular basis. He stood in the doorway as she moved around the room, getting a bowl from the cabinet and a pan from the stove, then finally turning and seeing him standing there.

"Oh, hey, Mike, I didn't realize you were back from your run," she said, and Mike could have sworn she looked embarrassed.

"I just got back and heard some beautiful music in the kitchen and had to come and see what was up." Mike gave her a big grin, feeling his heart swell a little when she fluttered her eyelashes at him. "Did you sleep well? Have any memories?" Mike asked her hesitantly. He didn't want to push her but wanted to know.

"I don't remember having a dream at all," she said, still moving around and getting the table set for breakfast.

"Do you know who the president is?" Mike asked her.

"I think it's Barack Obama?" She looked at him with questioning eyes.

"Yes, it is. I wonder what else we can do to help you start to remember things?" Mike said out loud. "I have great hope that it's not a long term thing, but I don't have much experience in amnesia. Did they make a follow up appointment for you to see a doctor about the amnesia?"

"I don't think they did. I was in such a hurry to get out of the hospital, I think I just forgot to ask. I can call them later," she said.

Mike knew it might be too much to ask for her to be remembering things at this stage in the recovery. Her physical recovery was going well – better than expected – so he felt bad that he could not seem to help her recover her memories as well. As they ate the eggs and sausage, her laughter at the simple jokes and chatter brought a smile to his face. Mike missed being part of the world and having a partner to journey with.

After breakfast, he thought it would be good for her to get out of the house and be outside for a while, since she appeared to have no trouble with walking or moving around on her own. After breakfast and a shower, Mike offered to show her around the outside of the house.

"I have fresh vegetables when they're in season. I lived on a farm growing up, and it's nice to have a garden. I have some tomatoes almost ready, and a few other varieties coming out now." Mike grasped her hand and led her out the door into the backyard.

She watched him carefully as he bent over to pick some red tomatoes and showed her the peppers that were almost ready. She felt the bright sun on her skin and put her hand up to shade her eyes as they walked on the path around the garden.

"You planted this yourself? You seem to have a knack for growing vegetables, and I don't see a lot of things dying on the vine. You have a way with plants." She smiled when he laughed at her simple joke. "Do the other ranches around here grow plants or are they cattle and horse ranches?"

"Around here are mostly cattle ranches, but I don't have any animals. I wanted to be able to leave again someday if I felt like doing mission trips – but I haven't quite decided if I want to do that again."

She wondered for a moment if he was talking to her or himself. He gave her a weak smile, then grasped her hand. "Let's head back inside so you don't overdo it."

Mike encouraged her to take things slow. She wanted to be outside, but he worried that she was still fragile. She worked around the house and did some light cleaning, but Mike was very cautious and always making sure she did not over do the activity. She was going slowly crazy because she was living without a point of reference. It made her want to scream. She was not an invalid.

At dinner that night, she talked to Mike when they were eating. "I'm afraid I won't ever remember who I am, even if my friends and family find me. What if I don't know who they are?" Her voice was shaky, and she could feel the tears welling up in her eyes. She didn't want to be so emotional, but it seemed like she could not control the swing of highs and lows.

Deep darkness shadowed Mike's eyes. They were a gorgeous contrast to his blonde hair. He reached over and touched her hand. "It's going to be ok, and you're stronger than you know. I can't believe how you have come out of the wreck and are already doing so much. I want you to slow down, and it's like you want to get through a bunch of steps because if you do you'll get your memory back. I wish I could take your pain and make it better, but you wouldn't let me anyway." He smiled at her and put his hand on her shoulder, then reached for her chin and lifted it to face him.

"I'm sorry, I just feel so sad sometimes." She sniffled and her voice cracked. "You're right.'"

"I want to make it ok, but all I can do is listen to you and support you," Mike said. "That is what I would have wanted…" He paused. "Only time will tell what you remember and how quickly. For now, take it slow and let your body heal."

They had not spoken about his wife since last night, but it was clear that she still lived within him and dwelled in his thoughts.

And she hoped someday she would find a love that strong, or maybe she already had one waiting back home – wherever that was? She just wanted to know what she did before, what type of job she had and where she lived. Basic things that most people take for granted. She felt sure that somewhere out there someone was looking for her, and she hoped that they found her soon.

To pass the time, besides reading books, she listened to the radio a lot. It made for good background noise, both talk and country music (the only stations that seemed to come in). She hummed along with the songs. Pretty soon, she had learned the words and sang along with them.

She wanted to learn about Mike, though, and tried to turn the conversations at meals to his family. Finally, over dinner the next night, he'd enough of her pestering and agreed to tell her about his childhood.

"Where did you live before you moved here, and why did you move here?" she asked.

"I grew up in this part of Montana, my father was a family doctor and my mother was his office assistant. They worked together all their lives. Jocelyn and I lived in Seattle, and I worked in the ER at University of Washington Medical Center," Mike said with a bit of nostalgic mist in his eyes. She could tell he missed doing the hard work of being a doctor by the tone of his voice.

"What does your brother, Chris, do?" she asked.

"He's my only family now that my parents have passed on. He works for the FBI and catches bad guys on the computer," Mike told her. "I'm going to call him tomorrow and see if he can help us find your past. I was hoping you might remember something by now or that the sheriff would have some news, but I think it's been long enough. I just thought about how much he might be able to help."

She clasped her hands together and smiled. Her sweet smile lit up the entire kitchen, and he felt like he'd just won the lottery with his simple statement. She looked at him for a long time, just staring at him and he wondered what was going through her mind. Suddenly, she jumped up and hugged him, and gave him a quick peck on the cheek. "If you think he can help, that would be awesome! I want to find out where I belong," she said, then just as quickly, she sat back down and started eating again.

The warmth of her kiss moved through his body, and the sparks from her touch were hard to shake. He smiled in return and bowed his head to keep from getting up and stroking her hair, holding her close, and telling her it would be ok. He needed to maintain his distance because when she did find her past, he wasn't sure she'd be available.

The next morning, they got up and walked back to the beautiful open field where they had gone before. Mike took her hand and led her over to the stones that were stationed like benches where the view of the landscape was laid out in the morning sky. The sun rose over the mountains and the tops of the trees sparkled from the dew. They sat quietly.

As she sat, she listened to the birds chirping. He lived in a gorgeous place, and the quiet peace it afforded made her want to stay here. No wonder he came here to heal his broken heart, it was calming and relaxing. She stood after they had sat for fifteen minutes and motioned for them to head back to the house. She decided to build on her walking every day and probably would eventually start running, as well.

When they returned to the house, she showered and thought she would set out some of the breakfast items. By the time he got down from showering, she had breakfast ready, except for the bacon.

"How do you feel after the walk this morning? You were being kind of quiet," Mike said.

"I'm feeling really good, and I am a bit sad, but not too much. I have hope, even if I haven't managed to remember anything yet," she said.

"It's completely normal to feel sad, you feel like you lost something. I am confident you'll regain your memory, but it's ok to be that way." Mike reached over and patted her hand. "I thought of a name to call you, if you don't mind."

"Oh, really, what would that be?" She smiled, and wrinkled her brow.

He smiled. "Taylor."

"Why?"

"Yep, Taylor, because you just love singing her songs and I hear you singing all day, so I think it's only fitting to give you her name. You have an angel's voice. I really want you to have a name so I don't have to start calling you sweetie or angel or something," Mike said with a laugh.

"I guess that will be fine, and I really haven't thought about how hard it must be for you to have nothing to call me. Taylor, it is!" She sighed. Though she appreciated his attempt to make her feel normal, this was another reality check that she was living without a past. They ate the rest of breakfast in silence, and Taylor offered to clean up the kitchen. She was feeling great after her walk, and more energetic than before, so she didn't mind moving around instead of sitting around all day. She also wanted to go upstairs and read another medical book, if she could understand it. She had flipped through a couple of them, but they were over her head and didn't seem to have information about her condition anyway.

When it came time for dinner, Taylor had spent most of the day thumbing through the books in his library that might have information about post-traumatic amnesia and how to overcome it. She found very little and understood even less of it. Taylor was feeling very confused by it all. *When I recover from this, I am going to do something about making it easier to understand what is happening.*

"What's wrong, Taylor?" Mike seemed to enjoy saying her new name.

"I'm frustrated about not knowing what will happen, even though I have been reading all the stuff I can find about traumatic brain injury and amnesia." Taylor bit into her chicken parmesan that Mike had prepared. "Thim if goom, by theewaaay," she said with her mouth full, but covered her lips with her hand.

Mike shook his head at her. "Thank you. And to get your mind off the subject of your brain, I thought I would entertain you with stories about my life as a doctor."

He saw the relief in her eyes. He had a feeling she was tired of being the subject of scrutiny about something she couldn't control, and he knew she spent all day in the library reading medical books, which by any stretch of the imagination was not fun.

So, once they finished eating, Mike leaned back in his chair and started telling some tales.

"We had a patient in the ER that I have never forgotten, who came back almost like clockwork every month, to get his medicine for his diabetes. I don't think he had insurance, and he knew we would give it to him – the hospital had a policy about only giving a month's supply or something. So, he would inevitably come in on my shift. And I got to the point where I already knew the story he would tell me, but I had to interview him. I noticed that every third or fourth time he came in, it was with a new pretty woman who was doting on him and usually paid his bill. After about eight months, I asked the woman to leave the room, and I asked him, 'Why do you come in with a new woman every few months, and they just can't get enough of you and taking care of you?'" Mike paused. "This is after I was married, so I wasn't looking for dating tips, mind you."

Taylor smiled, and he could tell she was thinking that exact thing.

Mike continued, "I'll never forget what he said to me. 'I listen to them and let them tell me everything without ever talking about myself. Women want to be heard, and by the time they figure out that I don't have much of anything, I'm still the only man in their lives who has ever just listened to them so they put up with me.' The guy smiled and nudged me. 'I see you're married, but go home and listen to your wife without talking too much about what you want or did, and ask her to talk about what she did, and see if it helps – you know'. He winked at me and nodded.

"That was not the response I had expected, but I did what he told me to do, not that I needed any help with the "you know" part, but my wife was like a whole new person. Whoever thought a guy in the ER would teach me such a good life lesson?" Mike laughed. *Note to self, listen to Taylor more, even if she doesn't have much of a past to talk about.* He realized he usually just peppered her with questions, and then she stopped talking once he stopped asking.

Taylor had been listening intently. "That's a good lesson. I've read some fiction in the last few days and it seems that all the women want is for a man to listen but all the men do is direct them about how to fix the problem."

She continued to look at Mike as if waiting for another story, so he obliged.

"Ok, here's a story about my brother, who seems to always be getting himself in trouble. I remember when Chris was a new agent. He got a case to work on that was for some celebrity in Texas. Some fan was stalking her and breaking into her house. The FBI got involved because the stalker was building a bomb to detonate at one of her appearances. Now, mind you, this was about ten years ago, so he didn't have the internet on a smart phone, or easy access to lots of information when he wasn't at headquarters. Just a brother who he could use as a lifeline, I guess." Mike stopped because Taylor didn't look like she understood the reference to a lifeline.

"A lifeline is like when you're stuck and you don't know the answer, you can call an expert or someone who does know the answer. They use them in game shows," Mike explained.

Taylor nodded.

"Ok, anyway, Chris was spending all his time with this woman and she would get letters in the mail saying, 'I'm going to poison you, I'm going to kill you if I can't have you,' and they were all from different addresses. Chris kept trying to find out who the person was, but couldn't track them down very quickly. And then the letters seemed to stop. The FBI didn't know why, and they kept Chris on the case. I knew from just talking to Chris that he was getting too involved with her, and he might not be objective or let down his guard. I think they call it getting too close to the victim or something." Mike looked up at her and saw her listening intently.

"One night, they were in Seattle at a dinner party thrown by some of her friends. Everything went fine at the party, and they went back to the hotel room after. Chris heard her vomiting uncontrollably. He went to the bathroom and it was nothing but blood, and he called me – freaked out and not sure what to do.

I drove over there, but Chris was also smart enough to call the friend's house. They found rat poison in the trash can, so I was able to administer vitamin K to stop the bleeding and get her to the hospital for some blood transfusions." Mike took another breath.

"Why didn't he just call an ambulance?" Taylor asked.

"It was a very secret investigation, and they didn't want the press to know what was happening. He knew I could get there just as fast and take care of her, and do whatever was needed. She stayed in the hospital for a couple of days, and they told the press it was stress related. Chris resolved then and there to track the guy down, and never get personally involved with another one of his cases. He should have done a better job checking on the staff at the dinner party, and he never forgave himself for letting his guard down." Mike stopped and was quiet.

"What did you say he does now for the FBI?" Taylor asked.

"He works in the cybercrime unit and tracks down people on the internet. He's very good at it, which reminds me that I forgot to call him today. I'll do it tomorrow, don't let me forget. I'm really sorry," Mike said. Her hand made its way to his forearm to offer some comforting touch and she smiled at him. They held each other's stare for just a few moments, then Taylor looked away.

"It's ok. I like it here, but I just wonder what my family is going through not knowing where I am or what's going on," she said quietly.

* * *

"I don't give a damn about you!" she yelled.

"You can say that if you like, but you know you want me." He smirked. Then he grabbed her and pulled her close. "You're nothing without me. I have made you what you are."

Her anger was about to explode. She got nose to nose with him and growled, "What makes you think that? I don't need you, and I certainly don't want you." She pushed back from his grip with both hands, and he let her go, causing her to stumble backward and fall to the ground. She stood up as he watched.

"We'll see how much you want me when you're all alone, baby." He turned and walked away from her and out of the door. She stood up and

walked out to her car, her tears just starting to fall.

She woke up and looked over at the clock. 2:00 am. She had been having a nightmare and thrashing around in the bed with Brutus. In her dream, he didn't say her name and she didn't know his, but felt like it was a boyfriend and her old self breaking up, something from the not so long ago past. Mike had told her she would probably remember the most recent events first. She jumped out of bed and went upstairs to Mike's bedroom. She knocked quietly and hoped he would wake up. She cracked the door and said gently, "Mike, I need to talk to you."

Mike sat up with a start, and looked at the door. She knew she looked terrible, but she couldn't help herself, she needed to see him and feel comforted by him.

He jumped out of bed and ran to her. "Are you ok? What happened, did you remember something?" He stood in the middle of the room with no shirt on and his lower half covered by boxers. She glanced at his handsome chest, his dark brown eyes, and blond hair. The muscles in his arms and chest so sculpted she wanted to reach out and touch them. He took her elbow and gently walked her over to the bed, then sat beside her.

"I had a dream or a memory. I was fighting with a guy, and he was saying he made me what I was and I was going to be all alone." Taylor felt the tears starting again and raised her hand up to wipe them away.

"Did you hear your name or his name?" Mike asked.

"No," Taylor said. "I'm scared now, and I wonder what I left in such a hurry that day, because I saw myself getting into my car after we broke up."

Mike pulled her to his chest and hugged her. Some of the tension left her body just with his warm touch. "Would you feel better if you slept up here with me? I'll put some pillows between us." Mike released her, knowing if he held her much longer he would start caressing her and they would be making love in no time, but he had much more respect for her than to make her his bridge to getting over his wife.

Taylor murmured, "Yes, that would be great. You don't have to put pillows between us. I need someone to hold me after that awful dream. The guy was really mean. I can't imagine I was ever with a guy like that." Mike gently lifted the covers, and she crawled into the bed.

Brutus jumped into the bed as well and snuggled into her side. She was back asleep in a minute, leaving Mike with his thoughts. He enjoyed the smell of her body and then wondered if he was falling in love with her. He reminded himself that he needed to keep her at arm's length. If she was having flashbacks, she would get her memory back sooner rather than later, and what if she had a husband and family? He couldn't do that to himself, much less to her. When it was time for her to go, he promised himself he would let her go without a fight. She deserved to get her life back.

Chapter 6

The next morning, Mike got out of bed as usual to go for a run. He felt the need for a very long run with a very long cold shower after the fitful night of sleep he'd had with Taylor in his bed. She had slept soundly, and he was glad she had not experienced any more memories last night. He needed to clear his head and think about what he needed to do next to keep his distance from her so that he could keep his feelings in check.

He had lots of thoughts going through his head, and he ran for almost twice as long as normal.

When he returned, Taylor was sitting on the porch with Brutus, waiting for him. He thought about how content she seemed, even without all the luxuries like the shops and TV. How old was she? He thought about 25 years old. He was 35 and that might be too much difference in age, even if they could have a relationship. He was an *old man* to her.

"Where do you run?" Taylor asked him, as he sat down beside her on the bench.

"I run on the trails in the woods and on the roads and where ever my feet take me," Mike answered. "It helps me to clear my head."

They walked inside, and Mike headed up for shower. After the shower, he walked downstairs, and she had breakfast all done.

"Can I go running with you tomorrow?" Taylor asked.

"I don't think it would be good for you. It's only been seven days since your injury, and you should be careful. We can go for a walk again, if you're getting a little stir crazy in here," Mike replied. "Tell me about your nightmare last night, I think it's going to be a breakthrough."

"I don't remember names or anything like that," she told him. "Thanks for letting me sleep next to you; it made me feel better."

"Good," he responded.

***

Taylor was still taking naps in the middle of the day, and she appeared to be as fully recovered as Mike expected seven days after the accident. After she woke up from her nap, Mike walked into the kitchen where she had gone to get something to drink.

"I know I promised a walk tomorrow, but would you like to go for a walk now to clear out the cobwebs?" Mike suggested.

"Sure, it's still just a really nice day. Can we take Brutus?" Taylor asked.

"Yep, no problem. Let's go." Mike got the leash for the dog and they headed out of the house in the opposite direction they had gone before.

They walked along a slight incline, so they went slowly, but Taylor started to see how the mountainous terrain was much different this direction. They walked for about 30 minutes when they came to a cliff. Near the edge was a flat area, and Mike pulled out a blanket for them to sit on.

Taylor looked at the scenery, up at the snowcapped mountains that rose before her and inhaled deeply of the fresh, crisp air. Small flowers cropped up around them, some red, some yellow, and the green grass was soft on her hands as she leaned back on her arms to rest. The 30 minute walk had taken a lot out of her, and as Brutus licked her face, she listened to the water rushing in the creek below them in the valley.

"Are you too tired out, did we walk too long?" Mike asked.

"I'm tired, but if we sit here for a while, we can walk back. It's downhill on the way home, so I think I'll be fine," she said.

"This is the part of Montana I love. When I was a kid, I used to go out and help the ranchers with their cattle when it was time for branding. A lot of grazing land and places to see, with nothing in between. The land is just so vast you forget you have anyone around you. And it's so quiet you can hear your own thoughts, unlike the big city," Mike said.

"Is that why you came back here? To hear yourself think?" Taylor looked over at him, and saw him take a deep breath.

"The noise of the city was just suffocating. When Jocelyn died, I felt so much guilt. I still have some guilt, just not being there. But she encouraged me to go on the mission trips and help others, and I thoroughly enjoyed doing it. I feel guilt that I left her alone, that I was not there and she died. She was too young to die. She and I were supposed to live a lot longer. I felt so empty, and I didn't feel like going to work or even getting up for that matter. So, I quit my job and moved out here. I think I moved here to be alone to die, because until I found you, I was just waiting to die. I realized it the other day. I was just waiting for my life to end. I didn't even feel things, and now suddenly I care that you're ok, and that you get your memory back and that you like my cooking," Mike confessed.

"I love your cooking," Taylor said. He wanted her to do something, but she just looked at him. He'd probably said too much.

90 | Page

Chapter 7

Taylor was unsure what to do, she couldn't tell whether Mike wanted comforting or not. He was just sitting there without saying a word. All she knew was that in the days since her accident, her feelings for him had changed, and she wasn't sure what to do about them.

"I am thankful every day that you cared enough to stop." *He is the only thing in my life right now until I can determine what my plans are and how I'll survive.*

Taylor watched as the faraway look in his eyes slowly refocused. "I could not have refused to help, and I'll be with you until you decide you don't want me to help anymore."

"You have to stop feeling guilty for what happened to Jocelyn. I know you have to grieve so you can let go, but you're not going to change the past by feeling guilty about something you can't change." Taylor stood up and reached her hand out to Mike. The sun was starting to get low in the sky.

Mike leaned over and kissed her forehead, then they started walking back to the house.

As she lay in her room that night, the feeling that she was a burden to him crept into her thoughts. He was holding onto his wife for the sake of having something to hold onto, and the idea that he was just "waiting to die" made her cringe. He had to get back to the real world. Tomorrow they could go to town and see a movie or something! The urge to go upstairs and hug him close or just sit quietly with him was almost overwhelming. Her heart ached for his loss. It had been one year since his wife died, but he acted like it was just yesterday when he was talking about her and all the feelings he must have felt that day.

The night was eerily quiet. She kept listening for Mike to make some noise. She had a realization that he must know at some point he was going to lose her too, back to her old self once she figured out who that was. That must be part of the reason for the distance he seemed to be keeping.

Chapter 8

In the morning, Taylor got up and started breakfast. Mike came down from his room after his shower, and she wondered how he felt after their talk yesterday when they sat in the wilderness. He must still be feeling so much guilt, and she wondered how to comfort him. She felt a strong desire to soothe his pain, much more so because of the kindness he extended to her in her moments of need. The daily little things that Mike did, like making her dinner and caring for her when she was about her situation, were so endearing.

Breakfast was quiet, and Mike didn't say much, except to ask the normal questions about how she was feeling and how she slept.

The sheriff came by later that day, and he spent a long time with Mike, discussing the accident report and outcomes. Taylor sat with them but let Mike do most of the talking. The sheriff really didn't have any information yet. Taylor guessed since the sheriff and Mike were friends, he felt obliged to keep them up to date on what was happening. The sheriff explained that the state crime lab was overwhelmed and they had not run her fingerprints yet, and the VIN number review was still being worked on.

When the sheriff left and they were alone in the house again, Mike turned toward the stairs with a grim look on his face.

"Mike, wait," Taylor said. "Can you call your brother and see if he can help?" She hated that she was asking, because she felt like she could really get used to spending days and nights with Mike, especially if he would warm up a little like he seemed to when he was so concerned about her nightmares.

"Oh, wow. I'm so sorry, Taylor. I promised you days ago that I would call and I haven't. You should not have had to ask me. Come over here and let's call him right now. Nothing is more important than that, as much as I would like you to stay." Mike continued toward the stairs. As much as he wanted to hold her in his arms and caress her gorgeous skin, he had to hold back so she could leave when it was time. Whether it was two weeks or two years. He liked the way he felt around her and wanted her to stay. They walked up to his room, and Mike picked up his cell phone. Unfortunately, he got Chris' voicemail.

"Hey, bro, it's Mike. I have a favor to ask, and I need your help. It's important. Please call me back when you get this." Mike looked at her

94 | P a g e

sheepishly. "Taylor, I can't tell you how sorry I am. Please forgive me."

"I'm not mad. I got really caught up in trying to solve my own issue of amnesia, that I forgot you calling, so it's ok. You don't need to feel bad about it," Taylor told him, and she meant it. It had not been on her mind until the sheriff had sounded like it might be years before he got an answer. She didn't even really know how much help Mike's brother could be, but it was worth a try.

Mike told her after lunch that they would take out her stitches and that it might hurt a little. She was excited to not have them anymore; it meant she was healing.

Mike got out his doctor's bag, and she sat down in a chair to let him review the situation He got out his scissors and tweezers and proceeded to cut the first stitch and pull it out. Taylor's hand immediately went to the spot. "Ouch!"

Mike batted her hand away, laughing. "I told you it might hurt." Taylor squinted her eyes and put her hands under her bottom to keep from grabbing Mike's hands and scissors to stop it. Mike was a little gentler when he pulled out the next few stitches, then he told her they were gone, and he leaned over and kissed her head where the stitches had been. She was surprised, but he said, "I remember how scared I was for you, and this just reminded me of how precious life is. I just wanted to comfort you in some way, like you have done for me with my grief. I know I haven't been the best company lately, but I am working on it."

Taylor turned and gave him a hug. "It's ok, I understand." She stood there in the hug, and Mike took a minute longer to let her go than he normally did. "Mike, are you ok?"

He dropped his arms to his side. "Yes." He turned and headed to his room, looking back at her as he headed up the stairs.

* * *

The weekend came, and Taylor wanted to go to a movie. Mike obliged her, and they decided to see a romance one day and an action film the next. When they got to the movie theater, Mike bought the tickets and insisted that they get popcorn, candy, and sodas.

"You have to get junk food, it's part of the movie experience," he told her. And she loved the popcorn.

Taylor found herself sobbing at the ending of the romance, and Mike put his arm around her and patted her hand. She laughed at herself for getting so involved in the movie that she was emotional about it.

The next day, they decided to go to the other movie and the grocery store.

I would like to see the site of the accident, if you don't mind," Taylor asked him.

"Sure, that might be really good for you and help you remember. We can go today after we make a grocery list," Mike said.

Taylor wondered if she would remember anything at the accident site, since her burned out car had long ago been hauled away. Her only memory so far had been an angry one, so she was hoping something might trigger her better memories.

So, after breakfast, they set about making a list of things they needed. Taylor had no idea if she liked or didn't like things, so she just went with what they had been eating so far.

Taylor watched Mike being domestic and felt like hugging him. She had stopped thinking constantly about what life would be like when she got her memory back and how she would return to her family. Here was a man who had saved her life and let her stay with him while he was going through his own trauma, yet she could only think about how much she wanted to rub his bare chest and kiss his lips. He had a long and lean body that was very muscular in a runner's type of way, and she wanted to spend more time with him. She rubbed her hands on her shorts and looked at the floor to stop the deluge of thoughts. They got in the truck to go to town. Mike told her it was a 30 minute drive to the store, and that they would stop at the "scene of the crime" on the way. She was sure it would bring back a memory or help her move forward so she didn't have to always feel so lost. She had already had one breakthrough; maybe another one would be triggered.

They stopped after about ten minutes, and Mike pulled the truck over to the side of the road. "Here it is," he announced. Taylor opened her car door and walked across the road to look at the tire marks and the places in the grass where you could tell her car had burned. She stood there for a long time, just looking.

"Don't try so hard to remember, it will come back soon. You're doing great with everything else, don't push it," Mike told her. He put his arm around her shoulders and stood next to her.

Taylor started to weep at the great amount of loss that she felt. She was probably never going to find out what happened or who she was. Mike pulled her to his chest and gave her a hug and kissed her forehead. Taylor cried for ten minutes into his chest without Mike saying a word.

Once she stopped, Mike gently asked her if she was ready to go.

"Sure, nothing is coming to me, so let's go," Taylor told him. She sighed and walked across the road to the truck and climbed back in.

"It will come," Mike said quietly. "Oh, and I almost forgot, but I haven't heard back from my brother, but that is normal since he might not even be in the country right now."

The drive to the movie theater was quiet and again, Mike insisted on buying the biggest container of popcorn and drinks to consume during the movie.

"It will distract you from the destruction that Batman is about to wreak." Mike told her. "And it's important to the local economy that we purchase overpriced food at the local movie theater."

"Well, if you insist." Taylor laughed as they took their seats. She sat down and looked at the big screen as the movie started and the previews were rolling.

She hid her face in Mike's shoulder for most of the movie, peeking out to see what damage was inflicted and how Batman was doing.

"Is he going to end up with the woman?" Taylor whispered to Mike in the midst of the movie.

"I haven't been to a movie in over a year. I almost forgot they had them. I have no idea," Mike replied in a whisper.

Chapter 9

They made it to the store, and thankfully, it was not busy. The store was empty except for about five people, and no one even really looked at Taylor and Mike. They got their groceries, and as they strolled down the aisle, Taylor found a few other things she was interested in trying.

"What about some chili beans?" she asked Mike, holding up the can.

"Ok, sounds good." Mike said, not really looking over at her.

"Did you write down dog food for Brutus?" she asked.

"Yep, I'm going to go over and get it now. Whatever else you want, go ahead and get it," Mike told her.

She wondered over to the frozen foods section and found the bonbons in the ice cream section. *These look delicious.* She grabbed them and put them in the cart. Mike raised his eyebrows but didn't say anything, which Taylor thought was strange.

"Come over here, Taylor, I want to show you something," Mike shouted to her over the aisle separating them.

"What?" Taylor asked, walking around the end cap and stopping in front of the bananas.

He started picking them up like a phone and saying, "Sorry, wrong number," then picking up another one and repeating that over and over.

Taylor started to giggle. "You really need to get out of the house more." The store clerk was eyeing them playing around in the aisle. "Ahem, we had better get back to shopping or else we are going to get in trouble." She elbowed Mike, and he nodded and put the bananas down.

When they got to the register, the clerk asked Mike, "Hey, Doc, who's your girlfriend?"

Mike responded tersely, "She's not my girlfriend." The friendly, comfortable atmosphere they had been enjoying was suddenly deflated. He gathered their bags, and packed the items in the truck and headed home quietly. The 30 minute drive contained only music, and Taylor hummed along. She wondered why Mike was upset at the comment from the clerk.

When they got back, Taylor started putting away the food and Mike went outside to get some vegetables from the garden. Taylor made dinner and used the fresh vegetables Mike brought in with the fresh meat they had bought at the store.

"Why are you so offended that I would be considered your girlfriend? We were having a good time, laughing and being normal. Apparently we look like we get along, so what's the problem?" Taylor asked while they were eating.

Mike swallowed and then laughed. "You're not my girlfriend; you're too young for an old man like me."

Taylor looked at him and rolled her eyes. "Whatever, we are not that far apart!"

"Taylor, slow down. You have been here less than two weeks, and you have no idea when you'll get your memory back. At that point, you could have friends and a family who want you back. I have grown to like having you around quite a bit, but I don't want to get into a relationship that may change dramatically in two minutes," Mike told her. "I am sorry if it offends you that I don't want to rush into anything, but you should put yourself first and work on your healing."

Taylor had to admit that it made sense to not get involved, but it was a little offensive to be treated like she was too young or not good enough for a relationship with him.

She lay in bed that night and thought about lots of ways they could work on her healing, together that would release a lot of tension.

Chapter 10

By the time Taylor had been at Mike's house for eleven days, she decided she could go running as well as him. So she got up and left right after him, running slowly but surely. Mike was listening to his iPod and didn't even know she was behind him. He kept running for about fifteen minutes and Taylor could not stay up with him but she could see him in the distance. He ran to the top of a ridge then slowed to a walk and ventured out to the area where he could stand and see the vast wilderness of Montana.

Taylor came up behind him, and walked to the side of him, about ten feet away, to keep from startling him. She fully expected him to be happy to see her. He turned when he saw her out of the corner of his eye, and his face showed frustration. He immediately pulled his ear buds out. "What are you doing out here?"

"I ran behind you. I was able to keep up with you and I feel just fine," Taylor told him with her chin lifted up in a show of defiance.

Mike sighed. "I don't think that just a couple of days after the accident you had, you could be 'just fine.' I just took the stitches out of your head, and your bruises are just now healing."

"I have been going for walks with you and improving my stamina. I feel like I was healthy and active before the accident so I should continue. And I'm so tired of being in that house all the time."

Mike knew he was overreacting, but he had been in a funk for several days now, and he could not seem to get out of it. But Taylor had a world that she didn't know about, and it was up to him to make sure she got back to them safe and sound. He needed to continue ignoring the way he was starting to feel about her, since anything else would cause both of them pain. "Touché. I haven't been a good host for a few days, trying to figure out what's going to happen and how I should handle it. But why? Today you kept up with me without much of a problem, who am I to tell you what to do?"

Taylor walked over to him and stroked his arms. He put his arm on her shoulders and turned to look out over the mountainous terrain. They sat down, and Mike told her about the mountains and valleys in the area. He described the different trees and types of plants that were around them. Taylor smiled and listened, glad he had decided to calm down and let her be with him, like she wanted. She hoped this was a turning point for him to join the regular world again.

After about an hour, they decided to return to the house, but Mike insisted they walk on the rugged trail to get downhill to prevent injury. Taylor knew he was still worried about her but she didn't feel any issues with the climb or the run. Either way, she gave in and walked down. On the road, they jogged back to the house.

Upon returning to the house, they went their separate ways to shower. Taylor spent some time braiding her hair to keep it away from her face. She was planning on working in the garden today. As Taylor emerged from her bathroom and walked to the kitchen, Mike was standing in there making them breakfast. Taylor was surprised at his demeanor. He seemed to have done a 180 degree turn around. He was smiling and whistling a song and cooking pancakes, but she also sensed his determination to keep her at arm's length. It was like he was trying very hard to be her friend and yet pushing her away at the same time.

108 | Page

Chapter 11

That night, Taylor had a hard time getting to sleep and kept tossing and turning. Part of her was mad because Mike was continuing to hold her at a distance. The rest of her was upset about the car accident. Her thoughts were on the side of the road where she'd been today and seeing the destruction that caused her life to start over again. She wanted to start now, and with what she knew now, because she understood that she might never recover. How would she deal with that?

Driving down the road in the middle of the day, she sang to the music blaring on the radio. She drove her Lexus LS460 at breakneck speed, like she was running away from something. Anger and intensity rushed through her as she absently petted her dog in the seat beside her. She didn't seem to care what the speed limit was, and when she looked down at her speedometer she saw she was going about 100 MPH.

She reached over and picked up the phone to read a text message. She swerved the car a little but corrected and got it back straight. The text was from someone named Bryan, but she couldn't remember what it said, only that it made her madder. Then she leaned back into the heated leather seats and put her foot down farther to get where she was going faster. Taylor saw another text come through, and she reached for the phone but the car responded to the slightest turn of the wheel and started to swerve.

She over-corrected this time, and felt the car grab some gravel and the back tires start to slide. She skidded across the road and turned the wheel back the other direction as she slammed on the brakes. Her car turned back but the wheels locked and she could no longer turn or stop the car from going into the ditch on the other side. There was a telephone pole ahead, and she was headed straight for it. No matter how hard she pressed on the brakes, the car would not turn from her inevitable fate.

Taylor sat up in bed, screaming. This was not a dream; it had to be the last few moments of her previous life. She caught her breath when she realized she was safe.

Five seconds later, Mike rushed into the room. "Taylor, what's wrong? Did something happen?" He squatted beside the bed, wearing only his boxers. She could tell he had woken from a deep sleep, as his hair was tousled—

perhaps he had been having a bad dream, as well.

Taylor remembered she was mad at him for his refusal to think of them having a relationship besides housemates, even though she was not sure it was the best thing. She responded by crossing her arms and gritting her teeth. "No, I'm fine. Nothing happened."

Mike tilted his head slightly, smiling, and grasped her hand. "Now is not the time to pout, Taylor. Tell me what happened."

"I had a bad dream," she said, sticking out her bottom lip.

Mike laughed. "It was another memory, wasn't it? You can tell me, it's best to get it out now or you won't remember as much in the morning."

Mike put his arms under her and moved her over in the bed a bit and crawled in beside her. "Taylor, honey, you have to work on getting better. I want you to get your memory back! Tell me what happened, it obviously upset you."

Taylor nodded her head. "I know." She fought the urge to grab his face and kiss him for rescuing her from her nightmare.

She then proceeded to tell him about the memory. She started crying when she realized how bad the accident could have been and how her stupidity had almost killed her.

"I am so stupid, Mike," she said, burying her face in his chest.

"Well, it shows us that you had or have a friend named Bryan," Mike said.

Taylor looked up at him and felt overwhelmed. He was a gorgeous man, more handsome than most of the heroes in the books she had been reading. And here he was, snuggled up in bed with her, comforting her, and all she could do was cry.

Taylor turned toward him, reached up and grabbed his face with her hands. "Right now, I don't care about my past. I want you." She closed her eyes and kissed him. She felt him hesitate then he pulled her closer and kissed her back. He was strong and powerful in his kisses, and as hungry as she was. He sighed as he gave in to the desire to touch her and pulled her down beside him as he cradled her head and continued to kiss her.

Mike was not sure how this would end, but he could not stop himself from letting it happen.

He could only hold back for so long, and here she was—practically begging him to give her all his attention. Mike continued to kiss Taylor, deepening the kiss by pushing his tongue into her mouth and inhaling deeply her sweet scent, almost like bubblegum. They were holding each other so tight they could barely breathe. As the kisses continued, Mike caressed her hair gently.

Taylor was overwhelmed with the smell of him and the feel of his powerful body over hers. He smelled clean and even though his hands were rough she loved the way they felt touching her body. Her body responded passionately as Mike kissed her and ran his fingers through her hair. She thought she would get a lukewarm response to her kiss, but Mike was obviously feeling the same level of emotion she was. His warm body covered hers, and she could feel his hard cock against her leg when he pulled her under him. She was breathing so hard from the all-consuming nature of Mike's embrace; she pushed him back for a moment so she could catch her breath.

Mike stopped kissing her and looked at her in a puzzled way. "What's wrong? Did I hurt you?" He pulled back further.

"No, and I know you don't mean to, but you're almost smothering me. Not that I mind, but I need to catch my breath," Taylor told him, with a little laugh.

Mike pulled back a little and smiled. "I guess I've been denying how I feel about you, and it's the middle of the night, and you needed me to comfort you." He laughed. "I do feel something for you, Taylor, but I don't want to stop you from going back to your life once we find out what it is. I don't want to tie you down." He sat up and pulled her to his side. "If I was a younger man, I would finish what we have started right here and not think twice about it. But I've already lost my wife, and I don't want to go through that again—nor do I want you to have to choose."

Taylor was surprised at the way he put his feelings out there. She thought about what he said, what if she did have a boyfriend out there? It was hard to know. "Mike, I want you and I'm very attracted to you, but I understand. I need you tonight. Can you stand to stay down here with me if we sleep in the same bed? I'm afraid of more nightmares."

Mike sighed. He was aroused and remembered how hard it was to sleep the last time he had her in his bed. He got out of the bed and stood up, not facing her. "Give me a couple of minutes to calm down, then I'll be back and stay in case you have any more bad dreams."

Chapter 12

Taylor lay in bed awake for the 20 minutes it took Mike to come back. He was dressed in a T-shirt and gym shorts over his boxers, and he gave her a shy smile. He ran a hand over his short blond hair and crawled into the bed and pulled her back to his chest, snuggling up to her, and kissed the back of her head. He didn't say goodnight or anything else, and Taylor wondered how hard it was for him to sleep in bed with her. If he had taken much longer, she would have come upstairs to get him!

When she fell asleep, her dreams were of Mike, not of a car crash. She slept peacefully, and did not even hear Mike leave the bed, but he was gone when she woke up. He was not upstairs either, but he had left a note on her bedside table, which she noticed when she came back down to her room.

You were sleeping so well, I went for a run. Be back soon. Mike

She sat back down in her bed and ran her fingers through her hair. She was not going to be able to continue fighting the fact that she really wanted to finish what they started last night. She wanted to run her fingers through his hair and feel him inside her, regardless of the consequences. She felt a warmth from her head to her toes when he touched her, and last night when they had kissed she wanted to touch every part of him and let him do the same. Why had she stopped him? When he was kissing her he had let go of the fear of loss, but the moment she had stopped to catch her breath he remembered what was at stake. She knew he wanted to make love to her just as much as she wanted him to last night.

Taylor grabbed Brutus, and they went to the kitchen to start breakfast. When Mike returned from his run, he asked if she'd had any more nightmares. The distance between them was back, just like the day before.

"What should we do? Should I leave to make this easier? I don't know where I would go, but I hate making you uncomfortable. It seems to be the only thing I am good at," Taylor told him.

"You're not going to leave until we know who you are and where you're going. I can control myself, as long as you don't have too many more nightmares. And I can get used to cold showers." Mike winked at her and smiled, but Taylor didn't feel like smiling back. She could only think about how hard this was for him, but when she looked at him across the table, she also knew she wanted him. She didn't care at this moment whether it was fate or something else.

"I still want to kiss you and take off your clothes – amongst other things, Taylor," Mike said. "But I'm going to avoid temptation. You're getting so close to knowing who you are, and then you'll be able to forget this place."

Taylor looked at him with tears in her eyes. "Do you think I want to forget this place? Is that how you think I feel?" Taylor realized she was being a little hysterical, but she couldn't help it.

Mike got up and pulled her to him. "Taylor, I know you don't want to forget this place, or me. I am trying hard to make it easier for you to leave when it's time." He kissed her firmly on the lips and pulled away quickly. "You're a hard woman to leave alone, you know?" He released her and left the kitchen.

The rest of the day, he avoided her. They both went about their work and ate together but with little conversation. Taylor decided she needed to take the bull by the horns and get what she wanted. That night after they cleaned up from dinner, Taylor bid Mike goodnight and told him she was going to do some reading before bed.

But she also thought out her plan for the next morning. If he was going to ignore her, she would see to it that he couldn't ignore her much longer.

When Mike got up in the morning to run, she got up with him and met him at the door as he was leaving. He looked at her kind of strangely, but realized he had little choice except to let her come along. She jogged with him to the top of the hill, and as they ran she could tell Mike was running slower to let her keep up with him.

When they reached the spot they had been to before, both of them sat quietly and didn't speak. They looked around at the beauty and stillness of the morning. Taylor thought about how gorgeous the mountains were, and how much she loved being out here in nature. She could tell he was intentionally not speaking to her as part of his plan to maintain his distance. *We shall see about that*. She scooted over on the rock and sat so they were touching legs. Then she grasped his hand and looked at him and smiled. He smiled back, and she reached up with her other hand and touched his cheek. They held the stare, and Mike glanced down at her lips. He saw Taylor's smirk and laughed. Taylor took that moment to kiss him, gently, on his lips.

They got up to leave and run back, but Mike reminded Taylor that they should walk down to the road because of the uneven trail. Taylor did as he asked, and they reached the house and split up to go get their showers without a word.

Taylor stripped down from her sweaty running clothes and quickly showered. She washed the grime out of her hair and skin, and then as she came out, she could still hear the water going for Mike's shower. She headed up the stairs in her towel and entered his room. She was changing their relationship. But she didn't care, this was what she wanted, and she knew she had an offer he couldn't refuse.

She opened the door to the bathroom and saw Mike in the shower. The glass square in the middle of the room showed him in his full glory. He was facing away from her, and she watched him scrub his hair, arms, and chest. He turned to rinse his hair with his eyes closed, and her gaze fastened on his bare chest. His manhood stood out at attention, and she got nervous. *Am I really going to make this happen?* Too late for second thoughts though, because Mike opened his eyes and immediately saw her standing there watching him.

Mike shook his head no, even as Taylor removed her towel and began walking to the shower, despite her moment of doubt. She opened the shower door and steam escaped as she stepped inside. He would give in to her. Although his head was shaking no, his body was responding to her. She hadn't come in here to get her back scrubbed.

Chapter 13

Mike gave up his fight, pulling her toward him. He kissed her again, but this time he was demanding. He reached a hand down to cup her breast, rubbing her nipple gently between his fingers. He wanted her so badly, he wasn't sure he that could calm himself down enough to make sure she enjoyed it as well. She was the first woman who he really wanted and who had gotten under his skin since his wife, and as he touched her gently he tried to push those thoughts out of his head. Should he risk letting her get under his skin? As he looked down at her, he knew this was the point of no return. Taylor moaned at his touch, and he pulled her into the water against him as he stroked her back. Taylor enjoyed his rough handling, and she pushed her body into his as they stood kissing in the shower. He couldn't stop, and he didn't think she wanted to either.

Then, once more, his rational side screamed at him to stop. Mike pushed her back and looked into her face. "Last chance to leave before we make love. Go dry off and get in bed, or go downstairs and we can pretend you weren't here." He pushed her toward the door. They were going to do this, either this morning or another, but maybe if they delayed it she would get her memory back and save them from some potential pain.

Taylor smiled at him and said a little sarcastically, "Aren't you the best at pillow talk? I'll be waiting in bed." She pulled a towel off the rack, wrapped it around her body, and sashayed out of the room.

Mike finished rinsing off the soap and tried to calm himself down. He thought for a moment about how he felt about Taylor, but right now, he was going to give her what she was asking for—and not make her wait much longer. He got out of the shower and proceeded to dry off and wrap his towel around his waist before entering the bedroom.

Taylor was in the bed waiting for him. "Took you long enough. Were you having second thoughts?"

"I was having many thoughts, but none of them were second thoughts. More like what I was going to do to slow myself down instead of devour you all at once," Mike said with a sly smile.

Taylor pulled back the covers and moved to the middle of the bed as he walked over. Mike grabbed her legs and pulled them toward him so she was lying horizontal, her knees bent at the edge of the bed.

"I know I won't last long once I'm inside that sweet body of yours, baby, I want you so bad." Mike slid his hands along the soft insides of her thighs, and willed himself to be gentle. He sensed her nervousness and realized they were both new to this in one way or another. He heard her take a breath and let it out slowly, as his fingertips trailed their way toward her center. Mike spread her legs apart and his fingers gently touched the outside lips of her pussy. He spread them apart and plunged one finger into her while his thumb found her clitoris and started rubbing in circles as he moved his finger in and out. He felt the desperate need to have her, to feel the warmth of her pussy around him and know it was him she wanted. He could drive her to the ecstasy her body wanted, and do it over and over again.

"Oh God, Mike. What are you doing down there?" Taylor squealed as her hips came up off the bed.

"Does that feel good?" Mike continued to rub her with his thumb and slowly moved his finger in and out, then pushed his face down between her legs and started licking her pussy. She wriggled on the bed as his rough beard stubble rubbed on the softness of her legs. He wanted to touch her everywhere, to hold her close, inhale the bubblegum sweetness of her soap. He felt like a teenager with his hormones raging, but wanted to show her how a man could give her pleasure that would satisfy her needs.

She put her hands on his head. "Stop, no don't stop, oh, I don't know what I want." Her head thrashed from side to side.

It didn't matter what she said; he was going to do this. He started out in the right place. As he licked and stroked her pussy, he could see the tension building in her body; she pushed herself further into his face and urged him to go faster. He continued to lathe her pussy with kisses, and he felt her getting tighter around his fingers, then the orgasm exploded through her body. She tensed up, and her buttocks rose off the bed as she clenched the sheets. "Oh my, oh my, oh my, yesssss, yesss…" she said as she slowly relaxed.

Mike pulled his face back and stood up. He took off his towel and laid it on the bed beside her. He stood between her legs, looking at her from her waist up to her perfect mouth, then to her closed eyes. He started rubbing his cock on her pussy, trying to push it inside her. The tightness felt good, and he didn't want to push too hard. He could still smell her pussy on his stubble, which aroused him even more. "Taylor, honey, open your eyes and look at me." Mike needed her to look at him, to see if their coupling affected her as much as it had affected him. Their relationship had changed with this act, and he was on the edge of falling in love with her.

Taylor opened her eyes and smiled, and he leaned forward to taste the softness of the skin on her neck. He pushed in a little, then pulled out, and then in more a couple of times, until he was able to give her full strokes with his hard cock. He knew it would be just a couple more strokes before he had to pull out since he didn't have any protection, but he also knew this was not the last time they would pleasure each other today. He pulled out after about ten strokes, and grabbed his towel as he came on her stomach. "Taylor," he yelled as his cum surged on her body.

Then he nudged her from her comfortable place where she had been enjoying their lovemaking by picking up her legs and moving them back to the middle of the bed. He crawled in beside her and started kissing her on the back of her neck and tasting the saltiness of the sweat from their encounter. "Sorry for the speed, baby. I have been thinking about that for a while now, and I loved making you come." He kissed her nose and caressed her breasts, but he felt goose bumps on her arms. "Are you cold, honey?" He immediately started briskly rubbing her arms. More than anything at this moment, he felt the need to protect her, and not let anything hurt her again. He had felt that way with Jocelyn, and he didn't want to lose Taylor. Taylor looked at him and smiled. "I'm not cold. I just got a chill thinking about how our lives have come together. I'm very happy to be in your arms right now. Are we going to spend the day in bed?"

He felt her warm smile all the way to his heart. "I don't know, there may be a few places in the house I would like to explore with you naked, but for now, I'm going to make you a very, very happy woman right here in this bed."

Chapter 14

They didn't venture out of the bedroom that day or the next—except to go for a walk in the garden, eat some food, and Mike went to the store for some condoms. They had spent a lot of time making love, but also a lot of time talking about what the future might hold.

"Mike, you're so wonderful. I want to stay in bed with you forever. It's so sweet making love to you, the way you massage my feet, drive me to climax over and over, and then you hold me when I go to sleep." Taylor lay in bed facing Mike, gently rubbing circles around his nipples as she spoke.

"Taylor, you're perfection. I want to drive you over the edge and fulfill your fantasies. I can't believe you're perfectly happy being here with me, but I'll make sure you enjoy it." Mike smoothed back her dark hair and kissed her faint scar over her eye, reminding himself of the reason they were there together.

Mike put his fingers between her legs and felt the wetness as he plunged his first finger into her slit.

"Mike, you're an animal!" Taylor teasingly pushed on his chest as she spread her legs for him to have more access.

"You make me this way, Taylor. I want to touch you all the time." Mike slid his lips down her neck and drew her nipple into his mouth. He continued to thrust his fingers in and out of her sex, and she arched her back, pushing her breasts into his mouth further. Taylor moaned as he brought her to orgasm, then made love to her.

He could not get enough of having her, touching her warm skin, listening to her sigh before she fell asleep, and tasting her lips. His need to satisfy her had not been satiated, but instead intensified with every moment they were together. He pushed the reality of their situation out of his mind, and blazed forward with open arms and heart for whatever the future was bringing.

After making love, they got up and showered, then walked down to the kitchen. Mike started making Taylor some cookies that he had picked up at the store a couple days before.

"Do you think it was fate that brought us together?" Taylor asked.

"Baby, I have told you before that it's like I just existed before I found you in your car. And then I couldn't leave you in the hospital, and I was going to find a way to take care of you if you wouldn't come to my house." Mike turned around and put a tray of cookies into the oven. "You have made me feel like living again. In between making love to you, I just want to take care of you. You make me feel like I have purpose again in this life."

Taylor couldn't believe he was being that open about his feelings. "Whatever happens, I want you in my life, Mike. No matter what. I feel like I am complete here with you, and even though I want to find my family, I want you to be part of whatever happens." Taylor looked up at him as he sat a glass of milk in front of her.

Mike kissed her on her nose. "Taylor, we'll work it out, ok? Don't worry now."

Mike ran his hand over her hip as they lay in bed that night. She turned her face to his and saw the desire in his eyes. He had a wonderfully lazy way of touching her that slowly brought the fire between her legs and made the tension build. He started drawing lazy circles on her stomach and shifted her onto her back so he could rub her nipples between his thumb and finger. She arched her back and closed her eyes as her nipples hardened. "Again, Mike. It's like my skin just starts to burn when you touch it. And the fire isn't quenched until you're inside me." Taylor moaned, and reached up to grasp his cock with her hand.

"Taylor, I just can't get enough of you." He dipped his head to pull her nipple into his warm mouth, as he gently bit down. Then he moved to her other breast and did the same. She spread her legs apart, and he moved his hand to the sweet slit and started to gently rub. She was wet again and smelled so sweet from her shower. He could smell her arousal as he pushed her lips apart and started to rub slow circles on her clit. He kissed her and pushed his tongue into her mouth, and she opened for him. He kissed her as she moaned into his mouth from the penetration of his finger as he continued to rub her clit.

She was so sweet, so delicious, and passion welled up inside him as he continued to push her toward a climax. He wanted to do this to her all the time, and he finally pulled himself away from her kisses to lick down her neck, breasts, and stomach until he reached the soft, wet center between her legs. They were in a 69 position, and as he pulled apart her lips and started to lick up her juices, she shifted to her side and took his hardness into her warm and soft mouth.

Mike continued to thrust his tongue as he rubbed her clit with his thumb, but with her mouth sliding up and down his cock, it was hard to concentrate. She took hold of the base of his cock and opened her mouth further to take it all in as she bobbed up and down, and Mike let out a groan. She continued, but suddenly slowed and sucked hard as she orgasmed from his mouth and thumb work. Then she started again, and continued to go faster until Mike warned her that he was about to come, but she just kept going and when he came in her mouth it felt like heaven. She stopped, and looked up at him. He lay flat on his back, and as she crawled up to kiss him, he said quietly, "Thank you, baby."

Then he rolled on top of her and gently pushed her legs apart. He brought his cock to her slit and started to push inside as he held her stare. She opened her legs further and smiled at him, and he pushed into her to the hilt. She sucked in her breath, and he started a rhythmic stroke until he brought them both to another climax. He pulled her to him as they relaxed after the lovemaking and kissed her once again. He didn't want to let her go, now or later.

The next day when Mike got up to get them some food, he had two messages on his phone. One call was from Mike's brother, Chris. Mike called him back and they talked for a few minutes about what happened and how Chris could help.

"The sheriff couldn't find her in any criminal database, but there are more places you can check, right?" Mike said.

"I can check her prints on a few systems, but it might take a few days. Some of those are kind of, not for everyday people, if you know what I mean. Has she remembered anything? Can't you whip out some of your doctor magic, Mike, and heal her?" Chris joked.

"I wish I could," Mike said.

"Oh, so it's a little more complicated than I thought. Are you sure that's a good idea?" Chris said.

"It's not a good idea, but I can't resist her. I've never felt like this, with such a fierce desire and possessiveness. I want to be with her every second. I want to protect her. Does that sound strange?" Mike confessed.

"Sounds like you're in love. Been there, done that, got the scars to prove it. Not going back… Anyway, send me the fingerprints, and I'll run them. Let me know if she remembers anything that could be a clue, and I'll see if I can use my magic computer powers to track down her lost history," Chris said. "Bye, bro, see you later."

They hung up and Mike realized that his brother was probably right. Just what he didn't want to admit.

The other call was from his friend, Jeff, who was going to be driving through the area, and wanted to stay overnight with him and see how he was doing. Mike's friend had been instrumental in his medical school days and his life prior to his wife dying. He sounded concerned that Mike had withdrawn completely from the world. Mike called him back and told him to stop by. Jeff agreed to be there the next day about 5:00 pm.

Mike almost didn't want to let another person into their daily routine, but his friend was a therapist and possibly could help Taylor find the lost memories. He went to their room where

Taylor was napping and woke her gently. Her touches and her words, her soft voice and her joy in life, those were things that he embraced and seemed to be bringing him back to his desire to go into the world and practice medicine again.

Mike resisted the urge to make love to her once again. He told Taylor they would have a guest for dinner tomorrow night, and asked if she minded if he stayed overnight in her old room. Taylor was surprised to learn Mike had a therapist friend, and even more surprised to learn he might be able to help her with her memory loss. She was not sure at this point she wanted to burst the bubble they lived in, but she wasn't going to waste a chance to get her past back. She was really glad to learn that Mike could send the fingerprints to his brother and run them through some other computers and try to find her. She got up and helped Mike get the information Chris wanted together, and they took the package to the post office and mailed it overnight to him.

When they got back, Taylor moved her things out of the room downstairs and up into Mike's room. She washed the sheets and cleaned house all day. They both were anticipating an interesting dinner when Jeff arrived, and Taylor was nervous about what he would have to say about her memory.

Mike appeared calm, but inside he was a nervous wreck, knowing that could mean their relationship would be subjected to trouble that he hoped they could make it through. That night, they made love in front of the fire in the living room and Mike wanted to possess her in every way. Taylor could sense the intensity of his feelings, and let him take the lead and just held onto him as he brought her to climax over and over.

138 | Page

Chapter 15

When Jeff arrived, Mike met him at his car and talked to him for a bit. Taylor suspected he was preparing him for her, because he did not know about her or about the circumstances surrounding her accident. They talked for about fifteen minutes before coming into the house together.

"Taylor, please come meet my friend Jeff."

Taylor walked into the foyer from the kitchen, and instantly she sensed that Jeff was surprised. He appeared to be taken aback, and she wondered how she looked. But she reached him and shook his hand. "Pleased to meet you. Come into our humble abode and make yourself at home. I have dinner almost ready."

"Thank you, I'll get my stuff arranged in my room and freshen up, and I'll be out in about fifteen minutes, if that's ok?" Jeff told her.

Mike stepped in. "Sure, let me help you to your room." He sensed Jeff's reaction as well, and wondered what Jeff saw that made him react that way.

At the dinner table, they sat and talked about what Mike had been doing and how his career was going before the accident. Mike told Jeff that moving here was the best thing for him, and that saving Taylor was the best thing that ever happened to them both. Jeff asked how Mike was managing if he wasn't working, and Mike talked about the stocks he had been studying and invested in to maintain his income. Mike had grown quite a nest egg, and had several million dollars of income that year from his parent's inheritance and his own savings. Taylor was surprised, and she had been wondering the same thing herself. Mike smiled at her and patted her hand.

Jeff asked more about Taylor's accident and memory loss, telling her that he was trying to see what he could do to help with her recovery. Jeff still seemed slightly taken aback throughout the meal, and Taylor was puzzled.

"Surely you've seen much worse cases than mine. Will I get my memory back?" Taylor asked him.

Jeff sighed. "It's just that I think I know who you are. I just can't believe it, so I'm trying really hard to make sure before I say anything…but all the pieces are adding up."

Mike squeezed Taylor's hand under the table. "Who do you think she is?" He was excited and scared at the same time.

"Lauren Jones, the lead singer from the band *The Five Sisters*. She has been missing since right around when you said Taylor had the accident. The story is, she broke it off with her boyfriend and was traveling to an unknown place to retreat from everything for a few weeks before the band started their North American tour. But a week went by with no one hearing from her, and her cell phone and credit cards haven't been used. The alarm went out, and people have been looking for her for the past week. They haven't found the little dog she supposedly had with her, either."

Tears filled Taylor's eyes. She was the lead singer of a band—and she was single, so she could still be with Mike. She was relieved Jeff had finally told them what he thought; now they could do some research and find out who she was. But her tears were also for the sadness at the realization that their little comfortable life was about to be knocked out of whack. She was scared Mike might not go with her.

Mike got up and pulled her out of her chair, kissing her tears. "Baby, don't cry, you're finally going to be able to find yourself, this is wonderful news."

"At least I'm apparently single." Taylor let out a short, bitter little laugh.

"I can't believe it took your friend five seconds to recognize me, and now I don't want to go be that person. I want to stay here, with you. Don't make me leave."

Jeff said, "I am so sorry, Lauren, I mean Taylor, I just wanted you to know. You need a little time to get a hold on all of this information."

"No, no," Taylor said as she shook her head. "I have to get my memory back. If that means I have to go back to the regular world, I know Mike will be there with me." She looked at Mike with questions in her eyes.

"I'll be wherever you need me to be," Mike said. They all sat back down and finished eating. Taylor asked Jeff some questions about the person he thought she was, as she really couldn't eat much more of her food. Once they were all done, she stood up and started clearing the plates.

Jeff bid them goodnight, and Mike and Taylor went up to Mike's room. Mike shut the door and pulled her to him. "Baby, this is the best news, and you're going to be fine. You're the lead singer of a band, no wonder I thought you had a great voice. Let's get started on figuring out what to do next."

Chapter 16

They turned on Mike's computer and looked up Lauren Jones on Wikipedia. The face of the woman on the page was Taylor, no doubt. With the scar from her forehead almost gone and her hair grown back in over her other cut, she looked exactly the same as the woman staring out from the page. They read about her and her band, *The Five Sisters*, an all-girl band made up of friends who had met in college. Lauren was originally a gospel singer, but the band played mostly pop and rock music.

Their number one hit, *Not My Problem,* was written by Lauren. She was 26 years old, and her birthday was June 25, so she was a Cancer. The page had recently been updated about her missing status, with a plea for whoever had information to call a number and there would be a reward. While she didn't have a lot of memories come flooding back, she knew in her heart that she had found the person who was lost that day a couple of weeks ago.

Taylor read all the information, then put her head in her hands and cried the tears of loss and of finding a new path but having to let the old one go. Mike rubbed her back, letting her cry. He was unsure of himself once she returned to the life of glamour that she was apparently so used to, even though he had promised to be wherever she needed him to be. She wrote down a lot of information on her history and what she had been doing. At first she was overwhelmed but quickly adjusted and started to get her bearings and did what she needed to do to get it together.

They made love that night, and Taylor clung to Mike as he brought her to another climax with his mouth and then as he sheathed himself inside her and drove them to a peak as she cried out his name. When she closed her eyes that night and started to dream, the memories started to flood back in. She remembered being on stage and singing. She dreamed of a concert in New York City and how they sold out the venue. She heard herself singing the song she wrote, *Not My Problem*, and knew the words. She heard the cheering crowds. She saw the others in the band, and knew they were friends as well as a band. This was not a nightmare, though, and she didn't wake up screaming.

When she awoke, Mike was up and ready to go out for a jog. "Would you like to come along, Taylor, and clear your head? I suspect you had some good dreams last night?"

Taylor got up and ran with Mike. When they returned, they ate breakfast with Jeff and bid him farewell. When Jeff asked Taylor what she was going to do, she told him she had not made up her mind yet. She wanted a few more days to think about it; she would go back to that world on her terms.

Mike's brother called right after Jeff left.

"I found out who she is, and wow, no wonder you're the way you are. She's beautiful, and available," Chris said.

"Yes, Jeff came through town last night and stopped by. I wasn't sure if it was too late to call you, but he recognized her and we figured it out last night. She's still trying to wrap her head around it," Mike said, smiling at Taylor as he talked to Chris.

"I knew last night but I thought I was letting you have one more night of peace before the world broke in. Call me if you need anything, and don't let her go. She is as good inside as she looks on the outside. I'm jealous." Chris hung up the phone to Mike's laughter.

Taylor and Mike sat at the kitchen table, and Taylor started to tell Mike about her dreams the night before. How she was remembering more about being a singer and this Lauren Jones person. She seemed far away, but Taylor was sure she was going to get her back. They'd been talking for about an hour when they heard a helicopter. They looked at each other and Taylor said, "Have you ever heard a helicopter around here?"

Mike shook his head and sighed. The helicopter was getting closer, and they got up to look outside and saw it land on the lawn out front. A woman with a short brown bob and Asian features and a man who looked like the "ex" from her dreams jumped out and ran to the front door.

Taylor stood frozen in place while Mike answered the door politely, inviting them into his house.

"Oh my goodness, it really is you! Lauren, Lauren, how are you?" The woman grabbed her and hugged her tightly.

Taylor stood still. "I'm sorry, I really don't know what's going on—where did you come from?"

The man spoke first. "Someone called in a tip this morning that you were here, and we flew an hour from Seattle to reach you. We haven't had any good information for the last week, and this person seemed so convinced you were here." Taylor turned and looked at Mike.

"Jeff?" Mike shook his head in disappointment.

Taylor told them to sit down in the living room, but the woman said, "We don't have time for that. You have to come with us, now, and see a doctor about your condition. The caller said you have amnesia."

With that, the man grabbed Taylor and picked her up. He started marching toward the door and another man came in the house to stop Mike from doing anything.

Taylor screamed, "Put me down, I am not leaving!"

Brutus came out of the kitchen barking at them, but jumped into the woman's arms when she said, "Come here, Pumpkin."

Taylor turned to see Mike trying to stop them but he was being held back, and Taylor screamed, "Mike, I love you, I love you, I love you," but her voice was drowned out by the sound of the helicopter blades starting up.

150 | Page

Chapter 17

They got Taylor and her dog on the helicopter and took off before Mike could do anything about it. Taylor looked down at Mike standing on his lawn waving to her and shouting something she could not hear. She curled up into a ball and started crying, and she cried during the entire flight back to Seattle. The woman's name was Shea, and the man was Bryan—her ex-boyfriend, who she had dreamt about fighting with. She refused to talk to them anymore except to ask where they were going.

When they got to Seattle, a doctor was waiting for them. She went into the room with the doctor and relaxed a little. Here was a man who could help her. She asked him what information he was going to give to the people who kidnapped her. The doctor looked alarmed at the fact that she was claiming to be kidnapped. Taylor explained the abduction, and the doctor wrote it down. He told her nothing from their visit would be shared unless she wanted it to be, but she needed to tell him exactly what she remembered. She told him about her two-week adventure with Mike.

Had it really only been two weeks? She loved him, she was sure of it. She didn't have his number, but she knew his full name, Michael Becker. After she finished, the doctor told her how lucky she was to have a trauma physician find her and save her. He also told her she was likely well on her way to getting her memory back, but he would work with her on a daily basis in private to help her make progress.

She agreed and went back to her "captors" who promised to get her home and let her spend some time where she could look around and see her own stuff again.

Taylor got to her house, and Shea came in with her. Bryan had dropped them off with a promise to return tomorrow to talk to her about their relationship. Taylor had to start thinking of herself as Lauren, because that was her real name, and Taylor seemed like a private thing between her and Mike.

Shea walked her through her large house, even larger than Mike's, and it was elaborately decorated. She apparently liked animal print. Lauren really did seem like another person altogether to her. As Shea showed her the rooms, it was hard to believe it was hers. It was getting late, and Taylor really wanted to call

Mike, but she needed to find out more about Lauren as well.

After the tour through the kitchen, bedrooms, and multiple living rooms, Taylor felt like she would collapse. It was so much to take in, and she dreaded going to sleep that night. She was certain she would find out more in her dreams, as her memories seemed to return and mesh together in her brain then.

Shea said, "Lauren, please have a seat at the kitchen table, and let's talk."

She was glad to sit and listen.

"I don't want to pry, and I know you're overwhelmed right now," Shea began. "The doctors told us you would need some time to re-acclimate yourself to your environment. They have great hope based on what you have remembered so far that you'll get your memory and old self back."

Taylor nodded her head. She really was not feeling too trusting of Shea, especially after the stunt they had pulled with the helicopter! Was that really just this morning?

Shea continued, "We were so frantic, and I'm sorry that we took you away like that, but it was necessary. We had no idea if he was a crazy person or holding you captive or what, How did you get to be there with him?"

"Mike found me on the side of the road, seconds before the car exploded. He risked his life to save me, and he's my hero. He wasn't trying to hurt me, he was helping me. What right did you have just taking me like I was a child?"

"I heard you tell him that you love him," Shea said. "I know you don't want to discuss what happened there, and I understand that you don't trust anyone right now, but you're in a safe place now. I'm not going to overwhelm you anymore tonight, and I'm going to leave a security detail here for you. The paparazzi will find out you're back soon enough and then they will be beating down your door. I know you don't remember how much of a pain it is to deal with them, so I want you to stay away from any press until you get a little better. Your mom will be here in the morning. She has been worried sick and is flying in overnight from New York."

Taylor understood what Shea was saying in a rational way, but the way she felt right now was very emotional. She wanted to talk to Mike, kiss him, and let him hold her in his arms.

Shea got up to leave, and then she hugged Taylor with tears in her eyes. "I am so glad you're back. We thought we had lost you forever, and I could not stand that thought about my best friend. It's hard to see you and know you don't remember, but you will. I love you. Sleep tight, and I'll see you tomorrow."

"Good night," Taylor responded, and tried to let her anger dissipate as she closed her eyes and thought of the cabin and Mike.

Chapter 18

Taylor went to her room, sat on her bed, and cried some more. She was without the man she loved, and she had been stolen away without so much as a kiss goodbye. She had no idea about Mike's phone number or address. How would she call or talk to him? He would not come here, she knew, without her talking to him and letting him know it was ok. That's just the kind of person he was. But how would she ever let him know it was ok if she could not talk to him? This was such a mess. She had everything a girl could ever want, and all she wanted was back in Montana!

Taylor cried herself to sleep that night and her dreams were of a girl who led a band called *The Five Sisters*. She dreamed of spectacular parties that had been held in her honor. She woke up a few times in the night because she was thrashing around in the bed so much. Finally, Taylor got up and took a bath about 5:00 am, spending a long time just soaking in the water. She put on her robe and walked through the upstairs bedrooms of her house, looking at the pictures of herself with others. She figured she would learn their names eventually, but just seeing the pictures reminded her that she was a strong and vibrant woman who could lead a band.

Her mom arrived at the house at 7:00 am, and Taylor could tell she had been worried sick. She looked pale and as if she had not eaten in days. She perked right up when she saw her. "Lauren, do you remember me? Please say that you do?"

"Mom, yes, I vaguely remember you," she said, lying to not hurt her feelings more.

Her mom hugged her tightly. "I knew you would."

Taylor hugged her back, sensing that she could trust her and wanting desperately to have someone as a rock in this storm she was going through.

Lauren's mom regaled her with questions about where she had been and what happened to her. Lauren explained as well as she could about what she remembered from the wreck and how Mike had found her. Her mom wanted to know more about Mike, but Lauren had to admit that she didn't know much about his history. She didn't want to disclose all that had happened between them.

She did tell her mom that she was in love with him, which her mother brushed off, telling her that Lauren had been in love before and would get over it.

"Why are you saying that, Mom? I thought you of all people would be happy for me that I finally found someone who made me happy." Lauren knew she was speaking loudly, but was just so angry she didn't feel inclined to control herself.

"Lauren, honey, you have been *in love* a million times, and you always end up getting hurt. Is this guy just another jerk who is going to break your heart?" Her mom stood and walked over to where Lauren was sitting.

"Mom, the last few days before I found out who I was were so wonderful, and even with the things that I have remembered so far, I don't recall any of the other ones being anywhere near that. Mike didn't know who I was, so he didn't care about me for my money like Bryan does," Lauren told her. "I want to go back to that."

Her mom looked at her and tilted her head to the side. "I didn't know you felt that strongly about him."

"I love him, and I'll be with him," Lauren said, matter of factly.

Her mom seemed hurt with her reaction, but it just reminded Lauren that she had been changed through this accident and recovery. "Mom, I realize I have changed some, but why did I not seem to sincerely be in love before?" Lauren asked her.

"You have always been so busy, and the men that you date just seem to come and go, you never really spent much time with them. Of course, you said you were in love with some of them, but then they were gone and it never seemed serious. It was almost as if you felt like you had to have a boyfriend around, but you never wanted to get that involved in the relationship. Bryan is the one you stayed with the longest, but he treated you pretty crappy. Then when you broke up with him, you disappeared. I just want you to stop feeling like your value is based on having a man around instead of the success that you have achieved with the band," her mom told her.

"That's the crazy thing. He makes me feel like it doesn't matter what I do, I am important to him. That my mere presence is what he needs. And I hate that he probably thinks I don't care about him now that I am famous. He didn't care what I did for a living, he was there for me and took care of me and wanted me to be healed on my own." Lauren looked around her house at the opulence that was missing from Mike's house.

"That sounds wonderful, but you need time to heal. I don't want you rushing into things," her mom said. "I know you don't remember but I rushed into a marriage with your father and it was a miserable ten years before I took you and left. I don't want the same thing for you, I want you to be strong and self-sufficient."

"I survived, and I am going to continue to be strong. Mom, I know you want the best for me, but so did Mike. He might not want to be with me anyway, now that I am famous. He was kind of living a quiet life before I came along."

Later in the morning, her doctor came over and Lauren spent a couple of hours with him going over her dream from the night before and what she had experienced that day. Lauren was determined to fight to get her memory back and find out how to get to Mike and have him back in her life. The doctor told her he would continue with the daily sessions so she could be ready for the start of her band's world tour in two weeks. Lauren was surprised that they expected her to perform that quickly after her accident. Maybe, if Mike didn't want to continue their relationship, it would be good to be working and forget about the gaping hole she felt in her heart at that moment.

Her mom promised to stay there with her for the next two weeks to make sure she was doing ok as well. Lauren felt like they were guarding her, to keep her from escaping. *Am I being a little paranoid?*

Lauren and her mom ate lunch together, and then her mom suggested that they go shopping to take a break and get out of the house. "You haven't been shopping for weeks; don't you miss it?"

Lauren thought about the quiet peace she had at Mike's log cabin. "Nope."

"Well, we can do some private shopping. I'll have your personal shoppers come over and show us the latest stuff to get your mind off of all these heavy thoughts you're having. Shopping heals all wounds, right?"

Lauren had to admit it sounded like a good idea to pamper herself a little.

Shea called after lunch and asked if the band could come over and talk to her. Lauren wanted to get some information from Shea, so she said,

"Fine. I need to know Mike's information though; can you bring that with you?" Shea said she did not have it, that it had been coordinated through the police and security detail, but she could help Lauren find it later.

Chapter 19

Mike woke up for the third day in a row on the couch downstairs. His house had been overrun in the last 24 hours by reporters from Seattle who had found out that this was where the famous Lauren Jones had been staying.

Mike felt like, once again, his world had been turned upside down. His sweet Taylor was a rock star. In the days following her departure, Mike had spent a great deal of time on the Internet researching Lauren Jones. What he found didn't really surprise him. The woman he knew as Taylor was a strong and independent woman. Her band, *The Five Sisters*, was moderately popular throughout the US and very popular in the Seattle area, which would explain why no one in Big Sky, Montana recognized her. Most of the locals listened to country music and Lauren sang mostly pop and rock 'n roll.

Mike looked back on that morning when they came with the helicopter and held him back as he tried to keep them from taking her and realized she probably had to go. It was in her best interest to get back to her life so she could regain her memories. The days they had spent before while she was recovering and they were

165 | P a g e

falling in love were a good resting time for her. He recognized now that he really had fallen in love with her.

It stung that she never called, because he had believed her when she said she really wanted them to be together even after she figured out who she was. Perhaps she and her ex-boyfriend had gotten back together. Mike didn't really want to think about that option but he had to admit it was a possibility.

What did surprise him was that looking through her history the sweet woman he'd come to know had toughened up a long time ago and was not as vulnerable as the Taylor he knew. Somehow she had broken down the walls that he'd put up after his wife died and he didn't want to admit it hurt him badly that she was gone.

Chris had been calling him every day, worried that this experience with Taylor might push them over the edge and cause him to do something to hurt himself. Mike knew he could never do that. Mike also knew he could get past this. He had spoken with Chris just last night about Taylor.

"Mike, you seem really down. Why don't you come out and see me in DC for a little while?" Chris said.

"I'm just waiting for the reporters to leave. This will die down in a couple a days. I've been thinking about doing another mission trip," Mike told him.

"I understand. If you're ready to immerse yourself back in the work, it's probably the best thing." Chris sighed.

"Thanks. I love you, bro. Talk to you later." Mike hung up.

The reporters stayed away from its front door, and he had enough food to wait them out for a few days. He figured this would be old news in no time.

So on that third morning after Taylor left, Mike thought about what he was going to do now that he realized he really did want to do something with the rest of his life. He had the skills to be a doctor, and he could help people even if he had a big hole in his heart. So he walked around the house and gathered up the pictures of his wife and Taylor's clothing and started boxing it up again.

Mike spent the rest of the morning cleaning up the remnants of the last two weeks with Taylor. Tomorrow he will call some of his old contacts and see about doing another mission trip. He still had his house back in Seattle, even though someone was renting it. Maybe, just maybe, if he went to Seattle he could see her and talk to her.

But then he realized they were from two different worlds and even though the accident had brought them together, she was going to go back to her family and her other way of life. Didn't he promise himself a million times in the past two weeks that he would not stand in the way of her going back? Didn't he remind himself over and over that she had something to go back to and to not get so involved so it wouldn't hurt so bad when that time came?

Even if she did call, it would be just to make herself feel better about what happened, so he would let her off the hook and be nice about letting go. She didn't deserve to feel bad about their relationship.

***

Around 3:00 pm, the girls from the band arrived. Each of them hugged Lauren and she could see they had been crying. She felt awful that they were so upset about her being missing and that she had not remembered them. But their sincere concern and obvious emotion with being reunited brought tears streaming down Lauren's face as well.

Lauren looked around at everyone after they had sat down and recognized each of the women but did not remember their names. They had been in her dreams over the past few nights, which gave her a level of comfort with them.

"We know you need some time to heal," Shea began. "But we also already delayed the start of the tour so we want to do what we can to get you back up to where you were before the accident. We thought that spending time with you and letting you ask us things and talking about the past would help with your memory. So, we understand that you don't remember our names, but we are going to try to remedy that."

Lauren shook her head and waited.

Shea continued, "I'm Shea, and I'm the lead guitarist and do vocals. We are best friends, and we started the band together. *The Five Sisters* has been together for five years, and we are a rock-and-roll band. You're the lead singer, and the face of the band. Next is Twilight Sands, our bass guitar player."

Lauren turned to the woman with long, blonde braids and a contagious smile that went all the way to her green eyes. It was such a warm and comforting face that Lauren immediately felt at ease and leaned toward her.

Twilight started talking, "Yes, and I am so glad you're feeling better. And getting parts of your memory back. I know that you'll get it all back. We are very tight as a band. You left after breaking up with Bryan—which, by the way, was a good thing in case he tries to tell you differently—and were going on trip for a couple days. You didn't tell us where you were going, so when you went missing, we didn't know where to look! We started getting worried after a couple of days with no texts and no calls. We were desperate when we could find no trace of you or your credit cards being used. I'm just glad that you're back, and I want to do whatever it takes to help out." Twilight's 5'10" frame was intimidating, but she walked over and bent down to Lauren and hugged her. Lauren hesitated at first, but the welcome exuding from her was hard to resist and she grinned as she hugged her back.

Lauren looked at her with tears in her eyes, realizing that they really cared a great deal for each other. "Thanks. I'm feeling better. And I appreciate you being here, even if I seem to just take it all in and not react much."

"Hey, Lauren. I'm Julie Lawson, the drummer, and I also do piano for some songs. I'm so glad you're back, and I want to do whatever you need me to in order to help you out." Julie had vibrant red hair, freckles all over her light skin, and bright green eyes that were as vibrant as her hair. Lauren waved at her from across the seating area. "Lauren, we all love you so much. Please know we are here to help you."

"Last but not least, I'm Samantha Hunt, and I'm the keyboard player in our little band. I joined the group about two years ago. I'm the youngest at 20, and I've written some of our songs. I'm also the one who is the boldest, so I'm going to ask—tell me about the guy you were with." Samantha's dark skin, ebony black hair, and brown eyes were a contrast to the rest of the team, but Lauren could tell she was the voice of truth in the group. If anyone would tell her straight about something, she bet it was Samantha.

Lauren took a deep breath and let it out slowly. "Mike saved my life; he is my hero, I would not be here if not for him and good fortune. When the car crashed on the side of the road, he rescued me from the wreck, and he took care of me. I can't stand to be here without him. He is my rock, and I am still pissed about Shea kidnapping me from there. I had every intention of leaving in a couple of days and coming here as soon as I could. I want to go back and be with him or have him here. I just can't talk about it and I need to know his address or his phone number or something so I can get to him." Lauren knew that getting too emotional about the situation was not good, but she was still raw with pain regarding Mike. And she hated them withholding information from her.

All of the girls turned and looked at Shea. She had tears in her eyes. "I was so worried, and was just doing what the security people said we should do just in case he had kidnapped you. I told you I was going to get his information as soon as I could."

All of them fell silent. Lauren felt bad about how they must have thought the worst and she now knew how much more complicated her life was than those two weeks in Montana. She stood. "Ok, well if you want to, we can go down to the studio I saw in the basement and play a few songs to see if I still have the voice. I hope they have the words somewhere." They all laughed at that.

Chapter 20

They all looked relieved, and everyone got up and they went to the studio and played for a couple of hours.

Lauren had not lost any of her voice, and she even started remembering parts of the songs. When they left, she hugged each of them and told them to come back tomorrow, even Shea. Lauren thought that she should give her the benefit of the doubt. Until tomorrow. If she didn't have Mike's address and phone number by then, she would start questioning everyone until someone gave her an answer.

After the girls left, Lauren sat with her mom and made plans for the next day. Bryan had called and wanted to come over and talk about their relationship, and Lauren suddenly felt the pressure of being ready for a tour in a couple of weeks. Her mom said she didn't have to talk to Bryan, but Lauren thought it would be good to get it over with. But first, she wanted to know who to talk to in the band about her relationship with Bryan so she could be on an even keel with him instead of being overwhelmed with his words and emotions. Her mom said that Julie was probably the best to talk to, because she and Julie double dated sometimes. Lauren called

Julie and asked her to come over for lunch the next day, and Julie was excited to help her out.

Lauren woke up in the middle of the night several times again; she knew this would be a chronic problem. She was having her memories return as dreams and visions, and it was overwhelming at times. But for now, she welcomed the thoughts and processes that were healing her.

The next day started out the same, except she went to the gym in her house that morning to exercise. Her voice was still fine and they could go on tour as long as she could take it. But it was a very physically demanding job and she needed to ensure she was in shape. Lauren supposed that was why she had a gym in her house to start with. While she was working out, she heard a song that made her immediately think of Mike, *Holding out for a Hero*.

Lauren thought about singing that to Mike when she got to call him later today! He would think that was funny.

After the gym, she talked to the doctors, and they were pleased with her progress and her ability to handle the changes that had taken place in the past few weeks. She was excited about the memory coming back, and even more excited at the thought of talking to Mike.

She even went shopping with her mom, although they had to go in disguise and try to not be noticed. She enjoyed getting out and she had watched some TV that morning to understand what was going on in the world. It was probably a good idea that Mike did not even have a TV with all the violence and craziness going on. Then they shopped at Macy's and found some great new jeans and makeup for Lauren. Lauren had to admit she loved the way the makeup made her feel like a woman.

Once they got home, Lauren took a nap because her lack of sleep the night before was starting to wear on her, and she knew the gals from the band were coming over.

Julie arrived for lunch like they had planned, and Lauren's mom left them alone to talk.

"Not all of my memory has returned, but what I remember about Bryan is not good. Did we always have an argumentative relationship or did something happen?" Lauren got straight to the point.

"I know it was not always that way, but the more popular the band got, the more jealous and crazy he seemed. He was always trying to put you down and tell you that you should do this or do that. It was hard to watch sometimes. I think the last straw was when he thought he was going to tell us where we could tour." Julie shook her red curls and picked up her sandwich to take a bite.

"He's not our manager or anything, is he?" Lauren asked.

"No, you met him in college and you've been dating for a couple of years but you wanted to get married and he kept putting it off. So when you started being more independent, he started pushing to control more stuff. You guys had a huge fight, and he was so mean to you. Then you said you needed some time away from everything, so you were going to some ranch or something in Colorado." Julie looked up at her. "It's probably better if you don't remember it. I just don't want you to get back with him, he was becoming very abusive."

"I dreamt that he was a singer too. As we became more popular, and he was not successful, was he almost spiteful?" Lauren asked.

178 | P a g e

Julie took a deep breath. "He was a backup singer for our band, but he was not that good. He started thinking he could make it as a singer with your connections, and when that didn't work, he changed."

Lauren frowned. "Ok, enough about me. Tell me about you, and your life. I remember things but it's not all put together quite right, so I don't know if what I think I know is really right."

"It's ok. Fame is great, and I love being part of this band. However, lately I have had some experience with the bad side of fame as well. I have some crazy guy who thinks he loves me who is stalking me and breaking into my house."

Lauren gasped. "What are you doing about it? That sounds terribly frightening."

"The police are working on it, and for the most part I forget about it unless I get a weird text, phone call hang-up, or a package in the mail. I am not worried, they will find him."

"I hope they do, people are just really crazy and unpredictable. You're welcome to stay here if you need to feel more secure and we can have a sleepover! It gets lonely in this big place, as I am sure it does in your place. Sometimes, when

I was in Montana and I had a flashback, I had to have Mike sleep in the bed with me the rest of the night because I was scared," Lauren told her. They finished their lunches and walked into the living room where Lauren's mom was sitting and reading.

"Shea said she would be over in a few minutes to talk about something with you," Lauren's mom told her.

The doorbell rang a few moments later, and the security guard let Shea into the house and led her to the living room where they were all sitting. "Lauren, I hate it that you're mad at me. You would have done the same thing for me. I'm *so* sorry, but I didn't know what to do—I was scared for you." Shea pleaded with Lauren to understand.

Lauren did understand, and the more of her past she uncovered, the more she could see where the drastic measures may have been needed if she was in trouble. Everyone's well-being was at stake if she was not returned, since she was the face of the band.

"Shea, I understand, but you took me away from the man I love, and I can't figure out how to get back to him."

Shea held up a piece of paper. "That's why I came over early! I got his phone number and address. Go, call him now! I'm sure he misses you as much as you miss him. I'm just going to get the studio ready to practice some more with Julie, if that's ok." Julie stood and nodded.

"Oh, I do forgive you!" Lauren grabbed the paper from Shea. Her hands were shaking, and she felt nervous about talking to him. But as she ran up to her room, her confidence grew, knowing that Mike promised to be wherever she needed him to be.

Lauren dialed the phone. It was the middle of the day, and she didn't think Mike would be doing much. It rang for a while then the voice mail system came on to leave a message. Lauren hung up. *Well, I should leave a message.* So she called again, but this time Mike answered.

"Hello?"

"Hello, baby! It's Taylor, I mean Lauren, and I miss you like crazy. I can't believe they kidnapped me like that. I didn't get to say goodbye to you, and I just want to be with you."

"Hello, Taylor or Lauren. Which name are you going by?"

"They call me Lauren, but I love it when you call me Taylor. What's wrong?" She sensed a hesitation in his voice that scared her.

"Taylor, I'm glad you called. I was going to write you a letter, but then I was not sure where to send it. I know you think you miss me, but you need to get on with your life and get your world and tour back on track. I've been inundated with reporters and media, and I just want to be alone right now. So I'm going to do some mission work to get away. Some friends of mine are doing a short trip to Haiti and wanted me to go. I wanted you to know it's ok to forget about me and move on. What we had was great, but it was just for a little time, and you have to go back to your life like I'll go back to mine."

"Mike, are you saying you don't love me? You don't want to be with me? I can't believe this. You're my rock, and the only thing stable in my life. Why are you doing this?"

"Taylor, this is for your own good. You don't need me to hold you down. I know you're a strong woman."

"What the hell is going on? I love you, Mike, and you don't care?"

"Taylor, I care enough to know you need to be free to do what you need to do right now, without me in the way."

"*In the way*, Mike? Really? That's how you're going to do this?"

"Taylor, I'm sorry. Goodbye."

"Goodbye, Mike." She hung up the phone, threw it across the room, and it shattered into pieces. So much for loving him; he had better things to do apparently. Damned if she was going to cry over him again today. She sat down for a few minutes and caught her breath and contained her anger. Maybe she was stronger than she thought she was. Nevertheless, this was not the end for her with Mike. She would see him. And they would have a reckoning.

Chapter 21

Bryan came over later that day, after the band was done practicing. They had gone over the songs, and mostly just had a good girl's session of reminiscing.

Bryan was dressed up in a pair of tight jeans and a button down shirt that showed off his strong chest and arms. His dark brown hair was cut close to the neck and over his ears, and his hazel eyes looked at her with longing. For her part, Lauren knew where the conversation would end, so she was unaffected by his attempts to be charming. Even if Mike tried to dump her, she didn't want to go back to Bryan. They sat in the living room, Bryan sitting next to her and grasping her hand. He rubbed her hands gently and looked over her injuries.

"Why did we have a fight and I decided to leave?" Lauren asked him.

Bryan pressed her hand to his lips. "That is the past. I was a jealous monster, and I was angry with you. Then I really lost you, and I promised myself that I would search to the ends of the earth to find you and tell you how sorry I was. Lauren, I'm ready to spend the rest of my life with you." Bryan knelt before her with her hand still in his embrace.

Lauren quickly pulled back her hand when she realized what he was saying. "I'm not ready to spend the rest of my life with you. I don't want to be with you, and I wanted to tell you myself. I wanted us to have an amicable friendship and not be angry with one another."

Bryan looked into her eyes. "Lauren, I'll wait for you as long as it takes."

Over the next week, Lauren and the band caught up on history and bonded all over again. They practiced often at Lauren's house, and also went to the studio and did set ups for the tour. There was little more than a week before they would have their first concert in over six months. They began practicing eight hours a day once they realized Lauren was healthy enough to endure that kind of torture. Lauren did not mind, as it kept her mind off of Mike and the cold shoulder he had given her. She thought about it a lot, and wondered if her mother was right about her getting over it. Did she really love him, or was it more of a hero worship? The only problem was that she missed him terribly and wanted to rush back to his place in Montana.

Lauren told the girls about how he had dumped her over the invasion of media and for her own good. They all told her it would be fine and that she didn't need him, but that was the last thing she wanted to hear. So she stopped talking about the breakup and started looking forward to the plan for the concert. She told them she wanted to dedicate a song to Mike during their concert – the *Holding out for a Hero* song she had heard on the radio. They talked about it and everyone was fine with it. Even though she didn't talk about the pain, they all knew Lauren's heart was with Mike, and she needed to dedicate something to the man who saved her life in more ways than one.

After about a week, Lauren could not stand it anymore, and she called Mike. He did not answer, but she left a message. "Mike, I just want you to know that I think this is a mistake to let each other go. I love you, and I want to be with you. I can't imagine that you're happy. We need to be together. It was magical." It made her feel better for a moment, but then she thought about how pathetic it was. In her moment of weakness, it had seemed like a good idea, but he never called back. That made her feel worse, but she understood; he was trying to make a clean break. He could he say he loved her, and that he was doing this for her own good. What right did he have to decide what was good for her?

A couple of days before their first concert, which was to be at a theater in Seattle as a dry run, *The Five Sisters* started media interviews to get the word out about their new tour. Lauren had not felt good enough up to that point because of all the practice and intensive work they were doing in the studio, so the promoters had held off. But she knew once it started, lots of the questions would center around Lauren and her condition.

She talked about how lucky she was to survive, and how thankful she was to God and to Mike for saving her. She tried to downplay the entire incident, since it seemed like a long time ago now, and she didn't want to cause any more issues for Mike or stir up any new interest in him. She showed her scar on her forehead; it had healed quite nicely, as well as the side of her head. She talked about having amnesia, and how alone and fearful it made her.

But she was determined to find a way to help those with more permanent problems from both car accidents and major injury – those with a Traumatic Brain Injury. TBI is a common problem for many people who have a concussion, vehicle accident, or are victims of violence. TBI can cause many problems, including physical, cognitive, social, emotional, and behavioral that more research and study could help.   Lauren announced that she would be creating a foundation – and the band would be donating part of the proceeds from the concert tour toward it. She gave out the website and asked people to go there and contribute. This brought in about $10,000 in donations on the first night, and her foundation continued to grow. She called her foundation, *The Five Sisters TBI Assistance Foundation*.

She was nervous for the first concert, because she still had twinges when she didn't know something or forgot what was supposed to happen. Fortunately, the night of the first concert went without a hitch. The girls in the band were so happy to have an uneventful night—a good start to their tour. Lauren sang like a canary, and her voice held out beautifully. She enjoyed the spotlight. It was like she played a part when she walked onto the stage. And the song dedicated to Mike was a hit – the crowd sang along with her and understood on the surface that she was thankful for her hero, and it proved to be a great ending to the night.

Since it was a local concert, they had some after parties to go to and then they all got to sleep in their own beds for the night. Lauren returned to her house at 3:00 am and walked up to her bedroom. When she opened the door, she was shocked at what she saw.

Bryan was lying stark naked in her bed, waiting for her to return. "Lauren, baby, I know you and I have been apart, but let's forget about that and make each other happy."

Lauren was too tired to fight with him. "Um, I haven't spoken to you much since I've been back and you think that's a fight? We are over. You're the reason I was driving on that back road in the middle of nowhere when I had the wreck! And how did you get into my room?"

Bryan got up and walked over to Lauren in all his naked glory. All Lauren could think about was how Mike had looked naked in the shower the first time they made love. She suppressed a giggle as Bryan stood before her and presented himself to her. She closed her eyes to keep from laughing out loud at his audacity.

"Lauren, forget that guy in Montana, you have me here, and I am very good at keeping you happy. I know exactly what you like. You forget that I was your boyfriend and I just told your security to let me in, so they obliged."

Lauren shook her head and walked past him. "Get dressed and go home. I'll fix the security issue."

Shocked and angry, he put on his clothes and left while she stood and looked out her window at the Seattle night sky.

Once she heard the door close, she turned and strode over to her phone. Surely she could call Mike and he would answer at this time of the night, just because of the element of surprise! As she dialed the number, her hands got a little shaky, and then her nerve faltered as the voicemail message came on again. "Mike, I love you. I want to be with you, and this is so hard. It's not getting any easier, and I know you have to be miserable too. I'm sending you a ticket for one of our concerts, and I hope you'll come and see us. I miss you."

When she hung up, she undressed and got into bed. The bed never felt lonelier than when she thought about her time in Montana. She allowed herself to cry—bawl, actually—and curled up into the fetal position as she fell asleep. She didn't want the hollow life of a rock star; she wanted the happy home life she had with Mike. Even at 3:00 am, it was undeniable that she was empty without Mike around, even just for the small talk about normal things. Why didn't he see that it was fate that brought them together?

Chapter 22

In the morning, Lauren thought about what tickets to send to Mike, and she decided to get him a ticket for the concert they were doing in Denver in a couple of weeks. That way if the mail had to get forwarded or he was doing mission work like he said he was going to do, it would have time to get to him. At least, she hoped it would.

They had concerts planned for the next couple of weeks in Portland, San Francisco, Los Angeles, Las Vegas, Phoenix, and then Denver. Their concerts were not the biggest news, but they were getting more recognition and respect for being a great band. They drew crowds of about 5000 people, and those fans were loyal. Some of them Lauren recognized at multiple places.

They did most of their concerts on weekend nights, just to draw bigger crowds. Plus, it gave them a chance to go home and relax a little during the week. The concerts were bigger this year because her disappearance had caused everyone to hear about *The Five Sisters*. It didn't matter, the entire band was very strong, and all the members supported each other.

So every night they had a concert, Lauren sang her heart out for the band, because she was back to feeling like they were a family. She had forgiven Shea, and she had most of her memory back to know how she felt about them before and just how much they had been through together. And Lauren sang her heart out for Mike, even if he couldn't hear her, because she believed he would be there in Denver.

As the night of the Denver concert approached, Lauren was nervous. What if he didn't show up? She would be crushed. He could come, but she also knew that he had stayed away for this long, so why did she believe he *would* come? Either way, she would do what she normally did—sing like she owned the place!

The night of the concert in Denver was perfect. The crowds had been growing and growing over the past couple of weeks, and Lauren was sure Mike would be here. She felt like he knew they were meant to be together, and it was not good for them to stay apart. She had not called him again, but her heart hurt for days after she called because he didn't call her. She promised herself if he was not there in Denver, she would accept the fact that he had moved on and work on doing so herself. But she didn't want to think about how that would feel.

Her life had changed so much over the past month. She really had become a new person. Even though most of her memory was back, she still maintained the down-to-earth person she had been when she'd woken up in Mike's cabin. She was not sure, but it seemed like fate had stepped in and brought them together. Before the accident she was a spoiled brat, and hard to deal with. Now that she understood the meaning of almost losing everything, she was much easier to get along with. She understood what was important. And her TBI foundation was at almost a million dollars in donations. That was something that the Lauren before the accident would not have done, but now it felt like she needed to do it.

She got on stage, said her usual welcome, and introduced the band. She looked into the crowd and could not see Mike in the seat she had given him. Her heart sank. She started singing and forgot about how much she wanted him to be there and be with her – she really loved to sing and make people happy with her voice. She sang for an hour, then after the second costume change, she walked out onto the stage and looked for him again to see if he had shown up late. No such luck. And he wasn't in her dressing room either.

So, as the concert started to wind down, it was time to sing her song to Mike. Her heart was in her throat, as she sang her song to her hero, and this time she had tears of sadness. Even though the crowd thought they were joyful tears, she could not hide her broken heart. Her voice cracked a little as she sang out, *"I'm holding out for a hero till the end of the night."* But, being the strong woman that she was, she continued and made it through. She gathered up her strength and continued to sing.

Chapter 23

A couple of encores later, Lauren had to admit it had been a great concert. They were gaining fans and people loved their music. What else could she ask for? She had her health and well-being and was the lead singer of a popular girls' band. What the heck, she knew what she wanted, she wanted it all! All the girls came together in the center of the stage as they bowed to the crowd. They all understood her pain, and she was tired of making them walk on eggshells about her broken heart. They hugged and walked off stage together, waving to the crowd.

She walked to her dressing room and made a mental list of the things she was going to do for the next couple of days. High on that list was going to the spa and figuring out what to do with the money they had raised. She closed the door and started to get undressed. When she heard the door open, she stopped taking her clothes off and yelled, "Just a minute!"

"I thought you might need some help getting those off," said a familiar voice from behind her.

She turned around to see Mike standing there in the door, and then he closed it behind him and locked it. She smiled. "I sure could!"

Mike was as gorgeous as ever; he had grown a beard and mustache in the last month and looked even more rugged. He had on boots and jeans, with a flannel shirt to complete the mountain man look. She ran to him, hugging and kissing him. He grabbed her tightly and kissed her thoroughly, then reached behind her back and finished unzipping her dress.

"Go ahead and get into more comfortable clothes, Lauren. We have some talking to do before we go any further," Mike told her.

She hurried behind the screen in her room, suddenly self-conscious, and put on comfortable jeans and a black t-shirt, as Mike made himself at home on her couch. When she came out, he patted the seat next to him.

He grasped her hands. "Lauren Jones, you're the most gorgeous woman I have ever seen, and if you're crazy enough to be waiting for me, I don't know why I am fighting it."

Lauren smiled at him. "That is what I thought, because I can't believe you haven't called me back or come to a concert before this," she whispered as tears came to her eyes.

"I give up. You win. I'm yours. I want to come to Seattle and be where you are. I'm going to start back to work some, but I have enough to make a living and I'm going to dedicate myself to our relationship. Lauren, I've been crazy about you ever since you woke up in that hospital bed, and I can't live without you. I've tried to for a month, and it's just not working." He shook his head and smiled like a man happy to be defeated.

Lauren grabbed his face and kissed him, then pulled back. "It wasn't working for me either!" She continued to kiss him some more.

Mike laughed and got up. "Thank goodness you let me in. Will you forgive my stupidity? I've been coming to your concerts for the last couple of weeks, and I could never find a way to get backstage to talk to you."

"Wait, you've been here all along, but you didn't tell me? All you had to do was just call me and let me know!" Lauren said, a little mad that she had been without him for no good reason.

"Well, I loved listening to you and hearing you dedicate a song to me every night. I couldn't continue to fight my feelings for you, so I was glad to get the ticket to this concert and the backstage pass." Mike felt the hole in his chest closing up, and the emptiness dissipating as he realized she would forgive him for being so stupid.

"You're so stubborn!" Lauren told him. "But so am I—or at least, that is what I hear. I want you to be the medical director of our TBI Foundation, you'll be perfect. I'll talk to the girls about it, but for now, I'm glad you're back." She put her arms around him, pulled him to her, and kissed him again. "Don't even think about leaving me. Together we are more than we are when we are apart."

Mike knew exactly what she meant, and he kissed her again. "Not a problem, I'm here and I'm not leaving. You're stuck with me. I love you."

Lauren pulled back. "I love you, too, baby. Now let's make up for some lost time."

Made in the USA
Lexington, KY
23 January 2019